A VISUAL NOVEL OF THE WAR OF TOMORROW

STRIKE EAGLES

JAMES P. COYNE

AVON BOOKS  NEW YORK

Acknowledgments: The author and editors thank the Department of Defense and the U.S. Air Force for their assistance, particularly with photos and diagrams. Many of the photos of Soviet equipment appeared in earlier issues of SOVIET MILITARY POWER, published by the Secretary of Defense. Also, photos and background materials from the following companies are acknowledged wih thanks: McDonnell Douglas, Boeing, General Electric, Hughes Aircraft, Northrop, Pratt & Whitney, Raytheon and Westinghouse. AIR FORCE magazine and Robert F. Dorr were also helpful, as always.

A VISUAL NOVEL OF THE WAR OF TOMORROW: STRIKE EAGLES is an original publication of Avon Books. This work has never before appeared in book form. This is a work of fiction, and while it deals with actual weaponry and combat technology, the people and events are products of the author's imagination.

AVON BOOKS
A division of
The Hearst Corporation
105 Madison Avenue
New York, New York 10016

Editor in Chief: Ian Ballantine
Series Editors: F. Clifton Berry, Jr., and Stephen P. Aubin
Art Director: Antonio Alcalá
Design Assistant: Amy Korman
Production Assistant: Barrie R. Levinson
Produced by: FCB Associates, Washington, DC 20005

First Avon Books Trade Printing: May 1990

Printed in the U.S.A.

DON 10 9 8 7 6 5 4 3 2 1

A VISUAL NOVEL OF THE WAR OF TOMORROW

STRIKE EAGLES

First production F-15E
aircraft, armed with four
AIM-7 Sparrow missiles
for aerial combat.
Cylindrical pods
underneath are the
LANTIRN night infrared
targeting and navigation
system.

Strike Eagle pilots and weapon systems officers (WSO) train on this simulator for attack missions and aerial combat as well. Enemy aircraft can be introduced into the training scenarios.

White-hot plume from the nozzles of an F-15's two Pratt & Whitney F100 engines pierces the darkness in a takeoff in full afterburner power.

Contents

Deploying Forward

Fighter Jocks Ready for War

They were a beautiful sight—four sleek F-15E Strike Eagles—flashing through the bright blue November sky high over Bitburg Air Base, West Germany. The aircraft wore the standard sinister dark gray-blue paint that told their main mission—night ground attack against high-value targets deep in the enemy's rear area. They were in perfect left echelon formation, stacked down. The flight leader, Lieutenant Colonel Tom Johnson, commander of "The Deadly Jesters," the 461st Fighter Squadron, glanced down to his eight o'clock position and liked what he saw: everybody tucked in tight and the canopies all lined up perfectly. "Looking good," he murmured to his back seater, Lieutenant Colonel Dick Elton, the weapons system officer.

"Of course," replied Elton. "Aren't they Jesters?"

He was not joking. The Jesters had a heritage and a reputation to live up to. Johnson reminded them of it at every opportunity. That meant doing the job right, every time. In competition with other outfits or among themselves. Including on-the-deck air-to-ground weapons deliveries at

14

Flight leader pitches right to approach for landing. His wingman (foreground) keeps station and establishes the landing interval.

night. Including hassling for quarters in air to air training battles. Including formation flying, arriving at your own base or somebody else's. Especially now, 2 November, when the training was over and the war had begun. Almost. NATO forces were at DEFCON 1, and the Jesters were deploying forward on a wartime contingency plan.

The 461st had a distinguished history, Johnson told them, going all the way back to World War II when squadron pilots flew Mustangs on the toughest missions of World War II, some of them in the same piece of sky they were flying through now. The squadron had returned to the States briefly after the war, been one of the first to convert to jets, and then returned to Europe.

Some great U.S. fighter jocks had been Jesters, including people like Sandy Vandenberg, son of the famous U.S. Air Force chief of staff. Sandy made a name for himself as a fighter pilot in his own right and ended his career with two stars.

The squadron was deactivated in the early sixties while with F-100 Super Sabres in Europe. It was reactivated as a Fighter Training Squadron at Luke Air Force Base, Arizona, in 1976, and was one of the first to be equipped with the brand new F-15 Eagle. In fact, it was so early in the Eagle's evolution, that the factory was still painting the aircraft "air superiority blue." Later, the color became gray.

The squadron reactivation was a classic, as

reactivations go, because former squadron members, some of whom had been in the unit in World War II, had traveled to Luke for the ceremonies. During the celebration, they regaled the young Jesters with war stories of the good old days, when a fighter pilot was, by God, a fighter pilot. They revealed secrets of fighter combat. They told outrageous war stories and even passed on secret recipes for the squadron mustard and the official squadron drink, "Panther Piss." By the time the veterans—"the survivors," they called themselves—left Luke, the new Jesters had a feel for the squadron's heritage and reputation.

The 461st compiled an outstanding record by training in the F-15 and trained its share of Eagle pilots, including Israelis and other allied students. The Jesters were first in the Air Force to be equipped with the F-15E. A year ago, the squadron was converted to an operational unit and deployed to Bentwaters Royal Air Force base in Suffolk, England. Now, Tom Johnson was leading a flight that was deploying forward to Bitburg. They made the 400-mile hop onto the continent in just 45 minutes.

From 20,000 feet, Johnson took in the dark green beauty of the rolling Eifel mountains below. Everyone called the area simply "The Eifel," and it was a lovely place to be stationed or to visit. A very short distance ahead was the Moselle River. Along its banks, German vintners in small towns with names like Bernkastel cultivated grapes that produced some of the finest white wine in the world. His eyes followed the twisting course of the Moselle as it flowed northeastward until it was obscured by low-lying haze. Tom knew it joined the mighty Rhine at Koblenz.

Picturesque villages, towns and castles dotted the peaceful countryside, linked together by a

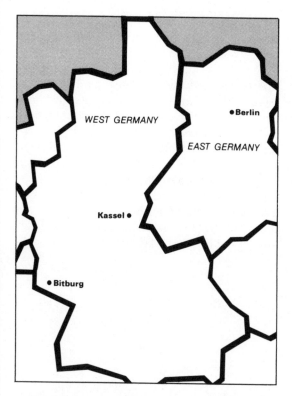

Bitburg Air Base is in the Eifel region, close by the French and Luxembourg borders. It was an assembly site for the German Ardennes offensive in December 1944.

17

network of fine German roads. Peaceful today, but tomorrow, he knew, once open hostilities began, this area would probably be under attack, and the Jesters would be flying from bomb-blasted runways or, more likely, autobahns, against Soviet forces in East Germany, less than 150 miles away.

Tom depressed the mike button on the throttle and checked in with the tower. "Bitburg tower, Jester One-One, flight of four over your station. Landing information, please." The F-15E was equipped with the HAVE QUICK frequency-hopping UHF radio. To preclude an enemy from jamming or listening in to transmissions, all HAVE QUICK radios hop to a different, preplanned frequency, ten times every second. Thanks to the magic of computers, there is no distortion or transmission breakup. And the frequency-hopping sequence is changed every day.

"Roger, Jester. Landing Runway 24," the tower operator replied. "Weather clear, visibility seven miles in haze. Wind two seven zero at eight knots. Temperature 34 Foxtrot, and the altimeter setting is thirty point one two. Report Initial." Looking through his binoculars, he watched the flight knifing through the afternoon sky. "Good echelon formation," he said to his assistant.

"Roger, 30.12," Tom replied. Dick Elton changed the altimeter setting from the standard high-altitude setting of 29.92 to 30.12. Glancing at his flight, Tom raised his gloved left fist until it was visible

Speed brake extended, F-15E main gear touches down on the runway in a textbook landing.

18

above the canopy rail to his wingman, First Lieutenant Sandy Scott, and moved it in a deliberate front-to-rear motion. He watched Sandy, the most inexperienced pilot in the flight, pass the signal on to Number Three, Pat Harris, deputy flight lead, who passed the signal on to Number Four.

With the same hand, Tom smoothly retarded both throttles until the RPM on the cockpit display read 75 percent. He exerted a little forward pressure on the control stick and the nose dropped. Since the F-15E trims automatically, he did not have to use the trim button on the aft side of the stick grip to apply nose-down trim.

Though the sleek bird did not decelerate appreciably, the whispering hum of the engines diminished somewhat. He then raised his hand again into view, this time with the fingers together and horizontal, and gave the "open speedbrake" signal by separating his thumb twice from his extended fingers.

After waiting long enough for the signal to be passed on, he gave the execution signal, a short head nod, and thumbed back the speedbrake switch on the inboard side of the right throttle. Immediately, Tom felt his bird decelerate as the big, flat speedbrake, hinged on its leading edge to the top of the fuselage behind the cockpit, was extended by a hydraulic actuator into the slipstream.

As the airspeed began to drop below 350 knots and the altimeter unwound at 3,000 feet per minute, he rolled smoothly into a 60-degree bank to the right. The sound of the slipstream, now disturbed by the protruding speedbrake, intensified.

As if locked in unison, the four Strike Eagles moved with Tom, each pilot keeping the same distance from the F-15 ahead of him and occupying the same plane as Tom's aircraft all the way through the sweeping, descending turn.

20   *F-15s of the 36th Tactical Fighter Wing are based at Bitburg AB. This is an echelon right formation above the ever-present cloud cover in Central Europe.*

Following standard procedure, he reminded Dick on intercom, "Oxygen, 100 percent." Each man flipped his oxygen regulator switch on the console from "Normal" to "100 Pct." Immediately, they began to hear the dry, rasping sound of their breathing on open mike intercom.

Using Spangdahlem, Bitburg's sister U.S. air base to the northeast, as a landmark, and staying well clear of Spang's airspace; Tom gauged the turn and the descent. He flew so that the flight would arrive simultaneously at the initial point three miles from the end of the runway, at the precise traffic pattern altitude, 2,500 feet indicated, at initial leg airspeed, 300 knots.

He signaled for speedbrakes again. On his head nod, all four pilots retracted them. He rolled smoothly out of the turn on a heading of 240. Altitude was 2,500, airspeed 300. He smoothly added power to maintain 300 knots. Bitburg was dead ahead and he was looking right down Runway 24. The inertial navigation system readings, as well as the TACAN navigation radio indications, displayed on the Head Up Display in the windscreen, showed the distance to be three miles. Perfect.

"Bitburg tower, Jester One-One initial."

"Roger, Jester One-One. Wind 270 at seven knots." Still watching the flight through his binoculars, and making sure he was not transmitting over the airwaves, the tower operator said "Good entry."

"One-One," Tom answered, and released the mike button. "How do they look?" he asked. Dick looked to the left. "Perfect," he said. The air was smooth as glass. Tom scanned the sky ahead, behind, above and below, and then glanced to the sides of the flight, checking for other aircraft. Even though they had been cleared into the traffic pattern, it was his responsibility to be sure another aircraft was not on a collision course with them.

Tom raised his hand once again. This time it was clenched into a fist, with the index finger pointing straight up. He made a rotating motion with the finger, then pulled it into the clenched fist and extended four fingers. They would take a four-second interval between aircraft on the break.

Bitburg Air Base was under the nose. Without looking, he knew the signal had been passed on to the other flight members.

In the back seat, Elton was scrolling through the prelanding checklist on the left display, checking especially that the armament and gun switches were off.

As he passed over the end of the runway, Tom briskly rolled the Eagle into a near vertical right bank, retarded the throttles to idle as he popped the speedbrake, exerted firm aft pressure on the stick and felt his G-suit tighten slightly around his legs and gut as the aircraft entered a three-G turn.

The pressure pushed him down into his seat,

Element of two of Bitburg's 36th Tactical Fighter Wing on downwind leg for landing on Runway 24.

not uncomfortably, and he felt his limbs grow heavy. Glancing down, he saw the airfield rotating counterclockwise below him. Looking ahead, he concentrated on keeping the nose level with the horizon so that he stayed exactly at traffic pattern altitude. While he could not see his flight members, he knew they were doing exactly what he was doing, four seconds apart.

"You're on speed, on altitude," Elton said. "You want 250 knots on downwind." Tom knew the traffic pattern speeds, but it didn't hurt to have Dick doublechecking.

Tom rolled smoothly out on downwind leg, parallel to the runway, which was just beyond the wingtip, and checked his instruments. Two

thousand five hundred feet and 250 knots. Hydraulic pressure, engine instruments, everything in the green. No warning or caution lights. Perfect. He reached for the small, wheel-shaped landing gear control handle on the lower left side of the instrument panel and moved it to the "Down" position, then moved the flap handle, at the base of the throttles, to "Down." He felt the deceleration as the gear and flaps pushed out into the airstream and heard the landing gear warning horn sound. The horn stopped when the gear was fully extended.

Though he did not have to add power, the other flight members did. They would fly a longer downwind leg before reaching the point where they would start the final descending turn.

Tom checked to see that the three landing gear position lights near the gear handle were green, the red UNSAFE light was out, the horn was silent and the flap indicator on the instrument panel showed the flaps were down.

When he reached a position just beyond an imaginary line drawn at right angles to the end of the runway, he started a smooth, continuous descending turn which would carry him through the base leg and onto final approach. "You want 150 knots on final," Dick said.

"Rog," Tom said, and called, "Jester One-One, turning base, gear down and checked, pressure up."

"Jester One-One, cleared to land."

24

Tom rolled in steeply and gradually shallowed the bank as he flew around the turn to final. He quickly scanned the instruments again. Everything good. Making sure his airspeed did not decrease below 180 knots, and concentrating on flying the aircraft, he asked again, "How do they look?"

Dick looked back up to his left and observed the positions of the other three aircraft in the traffic pattern. If they had entered the break exactly four seconds apart and had maintained the correct airspeeds, then they should be evenly spaced. "They're just right," Dick said. "Maybe Number Four is a little close to Number Three, but he's got time to adjust."

"Good," grunted Johnson.

In the tower, the controller, now watching without binoculars, commented, "Spacing is really right. This is a good bunch."

Johnson rolled out and lined up with the runway about a quarter mile from the approach end, 300 feet above the ground and at just above 150 knots. He crabbed the aircraft slightly to the right to compensate for the crosswind. The aircraft began to decelerate. He played the descent so he carried 150 coming over the runway threshold.

Sinking into ground effect, he pulled the nose up slightly to hold the aircraft off as long as possible. Just as they passed the little Mobile Control facility at the side of the runway, with the aircraft still in a crab (the F-15 landing gear is designed to land in a crab if wind conditions require it), the tires gently touched the runway in little puffs of gray smoke. A small "eeek" sound was audible in the cockpit. Johnson smiled.

"Hot damn!" said the young second lieutenant manning Mobile Control. "Right on the spot and a real squeaker. I grade that a One."

"That's Tom Johnson," replied the captain sitting next to him. "That's SOP for him."

Tom exerted backstick pressure to keep the nose high, letting the big wing area of the F-15E provide aerodynamic braking on the rollout. To make sure he did not get the nose too high and drag the tail, he used the W (centerline) symbol on the HUD, making sure it didn't move up to more than 12 degrees above the HUD horizon

First of the F-15E Strike Eagles, tail number 86183, during flight evaluations before the conflict began. External load is light: conformal fuel tanks and LANTIRN (Low Altitude Navigation and Targeting Infrared for Night) pods.

25

Prototype of the Strike Eagle version of the F-15, tail number 291, with load of iron bombs.

26

line. As the airspeed dropped through 80 knots, he smoothly lowered the nosewheel to the runway. Rolling to the departure end of the runway and turning off, he looked back and saw Number Two halfway down the runway, Number Three just touching down, and Number Four halfway around the turn to final. Just perfect. SOP, you might say. He retracted the speedbrake and raised the flaps.

Rolling off the runway, Dick changed radio frequencies. "You're on ground control," he told Tom. Tom followed the hand signals of a crew chief on the ramp near the runway, the Quick Check crew. They taxied into a clearly marked parking spot. Two crew chiefs ran under the aircraft and inserted red-flagged gear downlock pins into the gear actuation struts. Then they checked the tires for cuts or excessive wear, looked for leaking fluids or small holes caused by foreign object damage, and checked that no inspection panels had come off in flight. While they were doing this, the other three Jesters taxied into slots beside Tom. He held up two fingers, meaning he was on Channel Two, Ground Control, and they should dial in that frequency. When everyone had been checked, Johnson prepared to lead them to the parking ramp. "Jester Flight, Check."

"Toop," replied Number Two.

"Three."

"Four."

"Bitburg Ground, Jester One-One. Taxi and Park."

"Roger, Jester One-One. Make a left turn and pick up the Follow Me truck."

Tom added a little squirt of power to get his bird moving, retarded the throttles to idle, and depressed the nosewheel steering button on the front of the stick. Depressing the button increased the authority the rudder pedals could transmit to the nosewheel, enabling Tom to make sharp turns. Pushing hard left rudder, he turned onto the taxiway. The other flight members followed. They closed up the formation to a hundred feet between aircraft, each taxiing in a staggered position on the taxiway, avoiding the hot, shimmering jet blast from the idling engines of the next aircraft ahead.

"Looks like we had an audience," Dick said as they taxied by a blue official Air Force sedan with a colonel's eagle on the license plate.

"I recognize him," said Tom. "He's a good head. That's Colonel Crawford, the wing commander."

In the driver's seat, Colonel Van Crawford, commander of Bitburg's 36th Tactical Fighter Wing, waited for the flight to taxi slowly by and then drove carefully across the ramp to where the aircraft would be parked. Johnson's flight would be under his command while they were forward deployed at Bitburg.

He had watched the flight from the moment Tom checked in over the field and noticed the smooth, tight formation, the complete absence of radio chatter, the perfect entry onto initial leg, the perfect pattern spacing. All flight members had rated a "One" on the landing. Now, even their taxi speed and spacing were perfect.

"A very professional show," Crawford said to the colonel beside him.

"Based on first impressions, and Johnson's

reputation," said the other officer, Colonel Sidney Davis, the deputy commander for operations, "this looks like the right bunch for our special job. We'll know more after they've gone after that target tomorrow."

Johnson led his flight behind the Follow Me truck to their designated parking spaces on the big concrete Bitburg ramp, flanked by hangars and operations buildings. Other F-15s were parked there, but they were not Strike Eagles. They were superb air-to-air machines, but even though they carried a gun that could be used for strafing and could be fitted with bombracks, they were not designed to carry out the Strike Eagle mission.

A crew chief awaited each taxiing Strike Eagle and, using hand signals, directed it into its parking space. Tom's crew chief, in fatigues and field jacket, was one of the many females now assigned crew chief duties. She signaled with crossed wrists and clenched fists to stop. With the edge of her flat hand, she then made a throat cutting gesture, which translated into "shut down your engines."

In the back seat, Dick switched off the inertial navigation set, the radios, and the video and electronic gear. Tom moved the engine inlet ramp switches from "Normal" to "Up," moved the canopy control handle from "Locked" to "Up," and retarded the throttles all the way to the "Cutoff" position. The engines immediately whined down, and the strange silence that always follows engine shutdown, even on a noisy ramp, entered the cockpit.

Not speaking, letting the adrenalin drain from their bodies, each man unsnapped his helmet chinstrap and released the olive green oxygen mask bayonet fastener from its fitting on the right side of the helmet, letting the mask dangle from the left fastener. They released the mask hoses from the fittings on their body harnesses and unsnapped the leads from the aircraft oxygen supply to the other side of the fittings.

Next, they released the parachute male fittings from the shoulder-level female fittings on their torso harnesses, unfastened the lap belts, and released the torso harnesses' fasteners from the seat survival kits. Each man unfolded a padded green helmet bag from the map container on the right side of his cockpit and slipped his gray helmet, mask attached, inside, leaving the bag unzipped. They would entrust them to the wing Personal Equipment specialists, who would clean the masks, inspect them, wipe the sweaty inside of the helmets and hang them on specially designed pegs to dry.

While they were going through this ritual, the crew chief hooked a ladder over the left canopy rail. Tom stood up, stepped over the side onto the first rung, and backed the eight feet down the ladder. Dick followed suit. Each looked trim in his zippered green Nomex Air Force flying suit. Each man wore a circular shoulder patch emblazoned with the squadron emblem of the

29

Shoulder patch of 461st Fighter Squadron, the "Deadly Jesters."

At Bitburg, ground crewman uses power tug to fit F-15 into its hardened Tab Vee shelter.

30

Deadly Jesters: a gold harlequin mask under a comet streaking out of the sun, superimposed on a jet black background.

Walking from his staff car to the parked aircraft, Colonel Crawford looked closely at the two men. Johnson, just under six feet tall, stood confidently by the ladder. A shock of black hair, neatly combed, had been flattened by the helmet. His eyes were blue, his gaze as piercing as a laser. He had a strong chin. His body was well-muscled, but not beefy. He obviously kept himself in good shape.

"Right off a recruiting poster," Crawford thought. Next to Tom was Dick Elton, slightly shorter, but just as muscular. "They probably kill each other

at handball every day," Crawford mused. Elton, who wore glasses that gave him an almost professorial air, had features as striking as Johnson's—dark eyes, a good chin, and wavy brown hair, still plastered down from the flight.

"Have a good flight, sir?" asked Sergeant Jennifer Collins, the crew chief.

"Piece of cake, Sergeant Collins," Tom said, reading the name on her jacket. "You people certainly have great weather here."

"Only today, sir," said Jennifer. "The usual stuff—rain, drizzle, snow, sleet, low ceilings—is supposed to move back in tonight."

"Hey," said Tom. "Don't sound so glum. You're talking Strike Eagle weather. We've arrived just in time. That's the kind of weather we like. Nobody else is out and about in that kind of stuff."

"If that's your kind of weather, Johnson," Crawford interrupted, "you'll get plenty of it here. We're just enjoying this blue sky while we can. You and your partner can get into my car, if you like, and I'll take you to ops. Your flight members can ride in one of the squadron vehicles. You're all billeted at the BOQ next to the club."

The Bridge

Secret Mission for Lone F-15E

At 1900 hours, they gathered in the Intelligence Briefing Room next to the Operations Center. Captain Michael Falatchik, the wing intelligence officer, was already there, standing in front of a large wall map of Central Europe. Falatchik, a clean-cut young man wearing glasses, was dressed in the standard Air Force blue uniform with only a few ribbons on his chest. He exuded the usual Air Intell officer's aura of authority, confidence and superior intelligence.

Falatchik watched the aircrews in their flight suits take their places in the rows of seats before him. He did not fully understand them. At the Officer's Club, he had seen men like these before him now, playing their fighter pilot games and singing their fighter pilot songs. The aim, it seemed to him, always seemed to be to find out who could make the biggest ass of himself and have the best time doing it. Moreover, non-fighter pilots were never allowed to participate.

He had trouble understanding how these same people could be entrusted with an aircraft worth $25 million, much less one with wonder systems that practically require a Ph.D. to operate. Nevertheless, he had a grudging admiration for what they did. He listened to the stories they told at the club—bad weather, low fuel, occasional engine problems—and how the aircrews handled each situation. The trick, he realized, was for them not to get complacent. Complacency comes easily, because everything runs so well most of the time. But when the infrequent emergency takes place, things happen in a hurry. It's then that the aircrew better handle it fast and they better handle it right or they're dead meat—and suddenly the taxpayers are missing a very expensive machine.

For their part, the Jesters—and all fighter types —had their own view of intelligence officers. Not Falatchik in particular—just intell types in general. In past exercises, they remembered, the target never seemed to be exactly where intell said it was going to be, the defenses were always tougher than predicted and it never seemed to occur to the intell folks that somebody could get killed in this line of work. After all, the intelligence officer doesn't have to fly the mission.

Still fresh in Tom and Dick's minds was the last Libyan contingency two summers ago when intell had briefed "no fighter resistance expected," and the ragheads had put up 15 late-model MiGs. They were all shot down, but so were three F-111s which weren't expecting company.

After the flyers all took their seats in the small auditorium, Colonel Crawford faced the crews and started the program.

"As you know, we're virtually certain the war will start before dawn tomorrow. The Soviets have enough men and equipment in place from exercises just ended to pose a serious threat to the whole center area of operations. NATO's strategy is to hold as far forward as possible.

That means knocking out as much of their stuff as we can, as early as possible.

"You are going to make as close to a preemptive strike as we can get. You'll take off from Bitburg before dawn and fly low level to a point opposite tomorrow morning's designated entry corridor. No IFF (Identification Friend or Foe) squawk. Our own radar will be temporarily shut down in that sector so the enemy won't have the benefit of crosstell. Our Army in the Fulda Gap area will notify the command net of the first indication of enemy movement toward the West German border. Hopefully, that movement will take place before dawn. It will probably be tanks, supported by Soviet attack aircraft.

"You will wait for a codeword to be broadcast by one of the NATO AWACS aircraft that will be orbiting well back over our territory," Crawford continued. "When you hear the codeword, do not reply, just set course at high speed for your target. Avoid enemy fighters at all costs until after you have taken out the target. The CINC briefed me himself yesterday at Ramstein. If you pull

F-16 Fighting Falcons fought in the air battles on the first day. This flight of three deployed from home base to a forward operating location in Central Europe.

36

F-16s carried the weight of the air-to-ground daylight fighting while F-15s fought the air superiority battle. The F-15E Strike Eagles, flying in ones and twos, flew the tough night and in-weather strike missions, supported by F-111s.

this off, you will seriously hamper the Soviet thrust during the first part of the war. And if our side can hold in the Fulda Gap, we've got a chance of stalemating this thing before too many good people get killed."

"What is the rest of the Air Force doing while we're on this mission, Colonel?" one of the Jesters asked.

"As soon as the balloon goes up and your bird crosses the border, our side will be launching hundreds of birds armed for air-to-air work to take out the Soviet attack aircraft," Crawford replied as he pointed at the map.

"F-16s will be providing close air support to our ground troops and deep strike packages of

F-4 Wild Weasels and F-111s will be taking out the Soviet second echelon. By tomorrow night, hundreds of dogfights will have taken place and, hopefully, our side will be in control. After dark, all the Strike Eagles we can muster will be flying low and hitting high-value targets deep in the enemy rear."

"What is our target tomorrow morning, Colonel?" Tom asked.

"Chick, give 'em the details," Crawford directed, extending his hand toward the intelligence briefer. He sat down in his easy chair with "wing commander" on the back.

Falatchik took a deep breath. He had never briefed a real, hot war target before. "Your target

38

TR-1 reconnaissance aircraft, 12 miles above the battlefield, collected and transmitted information on enemy movements and concentrations.

is here," he began, "a long bridge over a river and railroad near the town of Meiningen."

Johnson and Elton exchanged glances. The tip of the pointer was only about 12 miles inside the East German border.

"As you can see," Falatchik continued, "this is a mountainous and forested area." He made a circular movement with the tip of the pointer.

"For days, we have watched them in their exercise, bringing tanks along this main autobahn through Erfurt, Gotha and Eisenach." The pointer tip traced the route, which was north of the target area.

"They will probably try to force the border right here, southwest of Eisenach" —— circular motion again—"and head in the general direction of Bad Horsfield on our side. Allied intelligence—we've got some pretty good Humint in this area—has located the equivalent of a blitzkrieg force near Meiningen. We estimate as many as 400 T-90s are hiding in this area, ready to move. They are probably intended to make a surprise thrust into our Army's right flank near the border. If you knock out the target, they'll be bottled up, and ground attack aircraft can pick them off."

On a large television screen next to the map, Lieutenant Falatchik called up a sharp image of the bridge. The Strike Eagle aircrews studied the image. It was a side view, taken either by an agent on an adjacent mountaintop, Elton mused, or by a reconnaissance vehicle equipped with a telescopic lens flying along the border. The bridge, two lanes wide and about the length of a football field, spanned a deep gorge. It was at least 200 feet from the bridge deck to the bottom of the gorge, Elton estimated. A railroad track ran along a small river in the gorge.

39

"The bridge is constructed of reinforced concrete," Falatchik said, trying to articulate his words carefully. "As you can see, a circular support arch extends out from each side of the gorge below the bridge and curves up to meet the bridge in the exact center. If you can hit it there, and breach it, it will collapse."

Johnson and Elton nodded.

"Now, some information on enemy defenses," Falatchik continued, taking a deep breath. "The Soviet army units you will fly over have the usual complement of SA-7 Grail shoulder-fired heatseeker missiles. They have a range of five miles. So far, we have no information on SAM sites. Too many trees and good camouflage. There are numerous ZSU-23-4 tracked guns. They have the old SA-13

Gopher self-contained tactical SAM. It has six missiles with a range of six miles, but it requires command guidance from the site. Because of the terrain, we don't think it will be able to track you. If your tactics work, you will be into the target before any of the missile units have time to react. Also, you have on-board countermeasures, so SAMs should be no problem."

"Right," said Johnson and Elton in unison, "no-o-o problem." There were some snickers from the other flyers in the room. Colonel Crawford looked annoyed.

Falatchik ignored the gibe. "Enemy aircraft," he stated, as he brought up an image of a needle-nosed Soviet fighter on the television screen. It was twin-tailed, like the F-15E, but heavy in the belly and not nearly so graceful looking.

"As you know," the lieutenant continued, "the Soviet Western TVD has over 2,000 fighters assigned to it, including this one, the MiG-31 Foxhound. This baby has true look-down, shoot-down capability and can engage multiple targets. For armament, it carries four AA-9 Amos long-range, radar-homing, air-to-air missiles. The Amos is credited with a low-altitude, head-on range of ten to twelve-and-a-half miles. The Foxhound also carries four AA-8 Aphids with a range of three to four miles. The Aphid is not nearly as good as the Amos at low altitude."

He changed images. "The Western TVD also has older MiG-25 Foxbats assigned. They were designed for high-altitude intercept work and probably aren't too effective in the intercept role near the deck.

"Probably not," echoed Johnson and Elton.

Falatchik plunged on. "The Foxbat carries six medium-range, radar-guided and/or infrared guided AA-6 Acrid missiles, or the new AA-11

Archers, medium-range missiles with active terminal radar guidance."

He displayed a third image. "You may also encounter the new dual-role version of the MiG-29 Fulcrum. The Fulcrum carries six medium-range AA-10 Alamo missiles. It's an all-aspect, look-down, shoot-down, radar-guided missile. The Fulcrum can also carry the AA-9 Amos and AA-8 Aphid missile. It has a 30mm gun for close-in work. Except for the MiG-25, these fighters are highly maneuverable and designed to dogfight. All of them have a long-range shoot-down capability."

Turning back to the map, Falatchik began to use his pointer again and said, "We have seen all three of these fighters in and out of airfields in the exercise area. Tonight, there are 10 MiG-29s here at the Waltersleben Highway Strip just south of Erfurt. There are twelve Foxbats at Haina. That's the closest strip to your target. Six more Fulcrums are here at Schloteim, and there are 10 Mig-31 Foxhounds at Arnstadt." His pointer traced a circle of small, relatively undeveloped airfields generally north and northeast from the

SA-6 (NATO code name "Gainful") is a low-altitude, radar-guided missile system. Its warhead consists of 80 kilograms of HE and steel fragments. Maximum effective range is 22,000 meters.

41

targeted bridge. The most distant field from the target was Schloteim, only 39 miles away.

Elton estimated the distance from the bridge to Haina to be less than twenty miles, or two minutes and 20 seconds at Strike Eagle speed.

"I presume all these enemy birds will be ready to leap off when the attack starts in the morning?" Johnson asked.

"You can bet your boots on it," Falatchik replied. "And, when they hear what you've done to their bridge, they're going to be pissed off!" Everybody in the briefing room chuckled. Falatchik was pleased that he had gotten a laugh of his own.

"One final item," Falatchik added, pointing once again at the map. "Escape and evasion. Long before this latest exercise took place, agents had established a safe haven near this mountainous forested area which happens to be only five miles southwest of the target. Today, the place is crawling with communist troops, but our agents have stayed in the area. So, if you're shot down, try to make your way there. A map and passwords will be given to each of you, along with an E

SA-9 (NATO code name "Gaskin") was used by Syrians against Israel in the Bekaa Valley. Minimum range is 500 meters, maximum is 8,000 meters.

and E kit before you go out to your birds in the morning. Okay, gentlemen. If there are no questions, that concludes the briefing."

"Thanks, Chick," said Tom. "It was a good briefing." He meant it. There had been some kidding back and forth, but the lieutenant had covered the mission pretty well.

Colonel Crawford stood up and looked over the eight Jester aircrewmen. "Okay, Johnson. You know the target and you know the situation. Now I'm going to tell you what your weapon is. You will employ the AGM-130 modular precision standoff weapon, two per aircraft. How many birds will you need, keeping in mind both the importance of getting the target and of the absolute need for secrecy?"

There were some low whistles from the group. Essentially, the AGM-130 was a 2,000-pound Mark 84 bomb with either a television or infrared seeker on the front end and a rocket motor on the back. It enables an attacker to launch the weapon a long distance from the target, usually lofting it by pulling up out of a low-level attack, or releasing

MiG-29 Fulcrum fighter- 43
interceptor carries AA-10
and AA-11 missiles, and is
a formidable threat in the
air superiority role.

it very high, out of a steep dive. The television picture the bomb "sees" is transmitted back to the launching aircraft, where it is viewed on one of the cockpit displays. Signals are then sent to the weapon guidance system, which adjusts movable fins to "fly" the bomb to the impact point. With this capability, the launching aircraft does not have to fly over the target, making it easier to avoid enemy defenses.

Johnson had expected the question. "One bridge, one Strike Eagle," he replied. "At least, in this case, two AGM-130s, placed right, should do the job. Because of the need not to attract attention to the attacker, only one aircraft should go. That will be Dick and myself." He ignored the groans from the rest of the Jesters. "We'll need one ground spare," he continued, "with the same weapons load, just in case something unexpected happens during start, taxi or takeoff. Once we get airborne, we're going, no matter what."

"Who gets to be the spare?" someone asked.

Johnson did not hesitate. "You get the nod, Pat," he said, looking at Lieutenant Colonel Pat Harris, the deputy lead for the flight into Bitburg. He had brought Harris along from England because he had been alerted that this was going to be an important, probably "hot," mission. Harris was the squadron operations officer, responsible for all the unit's flying activities and especially combat effectiveness. Like any good ops officer, he could fly rings around anybody in the squadron except Johnson. Harris had proved himself over the two years he had been in the Jesters, and Tom had already recommended him for a squadron of his own. Harris grinned happily at his backseater, Mike Gurth, who grinned back.

"Okay," Colonel Crawford said. "Those of you not going on this mission are excused. But be in the wing briefing room, suited and booted, for the ops briefing at 0500. We expect a lot of activity around here, including visitors from over the Rhine. When you fly, you will fly as a flight, under the command of this wing." The four excused Jester crewmembers filed out.

Immediately, the four Jesters who were left in the briefing room, the primary crew and the spare, went to one of the small flight briefing rooms down the corridor and began mission planning. They knew that in the munitions building, far down at the other end of the base, armament crews were assembling, or "building up," the components of their AGM-130s and readying them to be brought onto the ramp where they would be uploaded onto the two Strike Eagles.

45

Planning the Mission

Turning Plans Into Reality

Unfolding maps on the planning table, they looked over the situation and began planning their mission. Elton scanned the map.

"Here's a good spot to orbit," said Elton. "It's a TACAN radio site in the country directly west of Fulda. We have the exact latitude and longitude coordinates and altitude above sea level in the planning documents. We can crank them into the inertial nav system for pinpoint accuracy. Let's see. We'll probably have to take off on Runway 24, opposite the direction we want to go." Carefully, he measured the distance from Bitburg to the Gedern TACAN site, counting a 180-degree turn around to set course at 115 miles. The heading, he noted, was 077 degrees.

While Elton did the mapwork, Johnson got started on the rest of the flight planning, using charts from the F-15E Pilot's Handbook. For takeoff, he needed to know total aircraft weight. He started with the basic weight of the F-15E with internal fuel, 45,000 pounds. Then he added on the weight of the conformal fuel tanks, which fit against the side of the F-15E fuselage with

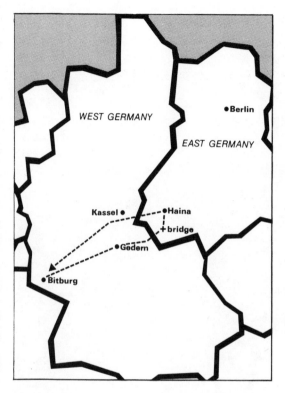

47

minimal increase in drag, and the weight of the fuel they contained. Next, he determined the weight of the LANTIRN (Low Altitude Navigation and Targeting Infrared for Night) navigation and targeting pods, the two AGM-130s and their mounting pylons and controller pod, AIM-9 Sidewinder heat-seeking missiles and four AIM-120 AMRAAM (Advanced Medium Range Air to Air Missiles), and computed a gross takeoff weight of almost 68,000 pounds.

Johnson then turned to another chart and computed a takeoff roll, without afterburner, of just over 5,500 feet. From this figure, he computed an acceleration check speed 2,000 feet after brake release, and a rotation and unstick speed. He

decided to exert backstick pressure on the stick at 155 knots. The nosewheel, he computed, should come off the ground at a slightly higher airspeed and, if he held the aircraft at a 12-degree nose-up attitude, they would quickly leave the ground at 180 knots. He had decided not to use afterburners for security reasons. The additional roar they produce, plus the bright, searing hot spurt of flame they give off, would be a beacon to the surrounding countryside that a Strike Eagle was taking the air. Nothing lights up a blacked out runway like an afterburner, and the Strike Eagle had two.

Now he had to compute fuel required for an all-low altitude flight. "You got time and distance figures yet?" he asked Elton.

"Right," Dick replied. "It's 108 miles to the holding point at Gedern TACAN." He pointed to the spot on the map. "Figure we cruise on out there at 500 feet above the terrain keeping it down to 400 knots so we don't make too much noise. That's 16 minutes. Let's assume we hold for about 15 minutes at 300 knots. Then, when we get the word, we start for the initial point. We look for the target on radar, keeping it in a freeze mode most of the time so we don't emit any more radiowaves than we have to. I think this tower near West Gersfeld, on the other side of the border, is a good IP."

He pointed to a tower on top of a mountain with an altitude of 3,789 feet above sea level. Actually, it was only a few hundred feet above the terrain at that point. But it would show up clearly on radar.

"It's exactly 40 miles from the holding point to the IP," Elton continued. "It will give us a good 30-degree aspect angle look at the target, enabling the radar mapping system to get an accurate fix on the bridge. I recommend we zip into the initial

During the night, ground crew members in protective gear service the strike aircraft.

49

point at 450 knots and 200 feet. That will take five and a half minutes. As soon as we make the turn toward the target, we accelerate to 540. If we stay at 200 feet above the mountainous terrain, we will lose line of sight on the target, but we'll be able to track where we are using the frozen radar map and inputs from the Inertial Navigation System and the Mission Navigation System. It'll be updating us all the way.

"It's 20 miles from the IP to the bridge. That's two minutes and twenty seconds. We'll come over this saddle"—he pointed to a drop in the contour lines on the map that indicated a drop in the terrain between two mountains—"about seven miles from the bridge. We'll have ample time—almost a minute—to get a lock-on, and we can launch the weapons at about five miles. They won't know what hit 'em or where it came from. Which way do you want to turn to come back out?"

"Just a minute," said Johnson. He went back into the charts to figure out how much JP-4 fuel they would use on takeoff, then on the different legs at the different speeds. He added up the figures with a pencil.

"Allowing for more than 15 minutes holding, and including returning to the base at high speed and low altitude, this whole thing takes less than an hour. We've got a lot more gas than that. We also have air-to-air missiles on board. Why don't we go after some MiGs?" Johnson asked.

Elton looked at him calmly, but his pulse beat increased. "Yeah, why not? Haina, that airfield with the Foxbats, is only 20 miles north of the bridge. We might catch some still on the ramp."

Pat Harris chuckled admiringly. "Great! Jesters make the first strike of the war, and get the first MiG kill!"

"Sounds right to me," Tom said. "I'll tell Colonel

Crawford what we intend to do."

Elton then sat down at the keyboard of the mission support system, which he would use to type the information they had computed into a Data Transfer Module. Tom would take the DTM to the aircraft with him in the morning and, before starting the engines, insert it into the DTM receptacle, just under the right-hand multipurpose display on the instrument panel in the front cockpit.

When the aircraft systems were actuated by the pilots, the DTM would program them with the information they needed. All the radio frequencies they would be using, including the HAVE QUICK frequencies, would be automatically inserted. The latitude and longitude of all checkpoints (waypoints), including the target, would be supplied to the navigation and targeting systems, with their altitudes above sea level. If necessary, three different routes, with up to 100 waypoints, could be included. The DTM also could be programmed to "tell" the aircraft what munitions were on board, and on what stations.

Detailed inspection by engine and airframe specialists ensure aircraft readiness for the mission.

51

"Let's see," Elton began. "Bitburg's coordinates are 49 degrees, 57 minutes, 22 seconds north, and 06 degrees, 33 minutes and 05 seconds east." Using this basic information, the Honeywell INS could keep track of the aircraft location within one-tenth of a mile. Updated with doppler radar information from the mission support system, the INS was accurate down to within a few feet. The INS could also be updated manually by the pilot as the aircraft passed over known checkpoints, or by TACAN and other navigational radios.

It took some minutes for Elton to enter the information into the automatic mission planning console. Assisted by the other three Jesters reading off coordinates, frequencies, weapon loadings

Weapons specialist checks 12-foot long AMRAAM missile before takeoff.

and other information, he programmed the DTM.

In earlier versions of the F-15, the programming had to be done in the cockpit, after engine start, and there was a delay of several minutes while systems came up to speed. Except for F-15s on alert; all those aircraft were "cocked." Before going on alert, the aircraft were started up and the systems programmed. Then they were shut down with a "stored alignment" in the INS. Cocked aircraft could be launched immediately after starting engines.

"Okay," Johnson finally said. "We're done for the night. We'll get an operations and weather briefing in the morning and an update, if there is one, from Intell. Let's head back to the 'Q' and catch some z's. Don't forget the briefing at 0500."

Each man checked into his BOQ room, showered, and was soon asleep. Johnson watched a half hour of the Armed Forces Radio and Television Network fare on one of Bitburg's two channels. The program was "Platoon," the Vietnam epic. "Geez," he thought, "this many kooks could never have gotten together in one platoon. In fact, I don't think they could ever have gotten out of boot camp." He turned off the set and went to sleep.

53

Cleared for Takeoff

Melding Man and Machine

The briefing in the morning brought the flyers in the Bitburg 36th Tactical Fighter Wing up to speed on the impending conflict. The Soviets were still poised to go to war.

Afterward, Colonel Crawford briefed the Jesters separately. There was no new information on the target. The weenies at USAFE said it was okay to go after MiGs. The "go" codeword for the mission was "Punchout."

Tom then briefed the crews of his own two-ship flight, leading off with a time-honored for-fighter-jocks-only insult: "Listen up, clods. I don't want to have to repeat this. Weather is 500 feet overcast and is expected to be the same in the target area. Visibility is five miles, with some misting, occasional rain and sleet. The temperature is 36 degrees Foxtrot and the dewpoint is 33. Conditions are ideal for fog. Let's hope it doesn't develop. The wind is 200 degrees at five knots. Altimeter is 30.00. Sunrise is 0740 hours local. The cloud tops are at 10,000 feet. We don't plan to get that high unless we do some hassling."

"You hope," Pat Harris said.

"Don't worry," Tom replied. "The forecast is that this stuff will burn off by mid-morning, making this base a good target for Soviet attackers. You will have plenty of visitors overhead and plenty to do later in the day.

"Tactical aircraft of the Western TVD are still deployed in the maneuver area," Tom continued. "Maybe we'll get one or two this morning. Last night, a couple of flights tickled the West German ADIZ. An AWACS IDed them and warned them off. No penetration or interception took place"

"Were they the usual radar ticklers?" Harris asked.

"We doubt it." Tom checked his notes. "They were two flights of four MiG-29s. The first one was detected at 2010 Zulu at Flight Level 450. The second was at 2115 Zee at 320. The intell weenies think they were logging some night flying and were vectored against the ADIZ to see if we'd launch. We didn't, and they turned home to those two long runways at Brand. They were probably also hoping to locate emissions from some of our new radar sites.

"Okay, you've got your takeoff data," Johnson concluded. "We're Jester One-One and Jester One-Two. You start up and taxi out behind me, Pat. If I don't get off for some reason, you go instead. If I do get off, you taxi back in and shut down. Let's suit up."

Word of their mission traveled fast after the morning briefing. Other Eagle drivers looked at them enviously as they strode into Personal Equipment in their Nomex flying suits and heavy laced boots. Johnson took his grey padded helmet off its wallpeg, put it on, fastened the oxygen mask and checked its operation and the operation of the built-in microphone, using the test equipment on the counter. The other Jesters followed suit. He removed the helmet and put it in the green

55

56

Multipurpose displays in front cockpit of F-15E replace the clutter of circular dials on older aircraft. Throttle quadrant for controlling the two F100 engines is at left.

carrying bag. He then donned his G-suit, zipping the legs up from ankle to crotch. Each man made sure the lace adjustments for calves, thighs and abdomen were snug. Then each used the test equipment to be sure the suit inflated as it should, with no leaks.

They put on their sage green winter flying

jackets and zipped them up to the black-and-gold checked scarves they wore at their necks. Finally, Tom put on his torso harness, specially fitted and hand-sewn so it hugged his body contours with exactness. In the aircraft, he would attach the parachute fittings to the top of the harness, and the survival kit in the aircraft seat would be

Four multipurpose displays dominate panel in rear cockpit, where weapons system officer plies his trade. Essential flight instruments and controls are here.

attached to the lower part. The fitting for the oxygen hose and microphone connections were on the left front vertical strap of the harness.

Like most men going to war, they didn't say much as they rode out to their aircraft together in one of the wing's "Bread Wagons." The birds were parked side by side in the almost total darkness. The whole base was blacked out. It was misty and they could sense the low overcast, invisible in the gloom as it hung over them. As reported, the temperature was in the mid-30s. It was winter in Germany again. The two crews parted and went to their aircraft.

"See ya on Channel Three," Tom called.

Sergeant Jennifer Collins walked out from under the shelter of the right wing. "She's ready to go, Colonel," she said.

"Well, good morning, Sergeant." He pulled on his flying gloves. "Nice to see you on such a fine morning."

"I know, a Strike Eagle morning." She was dressed in heavy cold weather gear. "I guess I prefer the other kind."

Tom climbed the ladder, placed his helmet on the left canopy rail and, leaning across the ejection seat, stowed the helmet bag in the map compartment. He checked the safety pins in the seat and made sure all the fittings and connections were secure.

He climbed back down for the walkaround inspection. The Strike Eagle looked deadly enough in its dark paint job, but the ugly AGM-130s, one under each wing, intensified the appearance. Tom inspected one, and then the other, using a small flashlight. Placing his gloved hands against the huge Mk 84 bomb casing, he leaned his weight against it to check the security of the suspension. Good. Only a minuscule sway.

"These babies are going to knock down a bridge

today," he told the sergeant.

Tom checked the explosive squibs in each bomb rack. The squibs would be electrically fired at the precise instant Tom depressed the pickle button on the control stick. They would unlock the hooks from the heavy bomb lugs and actuate the thrusters which physically push the bombs from the rack. Their rocket motors would then propel them to their targets.

He brushed the red streamers that swayed in the slight breeze as they hung from safing pins in the nose and tail fuses. He made sure the rocket motor was securely bolted to the aft end of each ugly 2000-pounder and that the sensor and guidance section was securely fastened to the nose. Tom looked closely to be sure the bomb's fins had not been damaged during installation nor obstructed by the aircraft structure. Two white AIM-9M all-aspect Sidewinder missiles, heatseekers, were mounted on each pylon, above the AGM-130s. He carefully removed the rubberized nose covers from each missile and checked that the clear infrared seeker head was not cracked or clouded. Then he replaced the covers. They would be removed just before takeoff by the armorers. He gave the saw-toothed metal disks on the corner of each missile's rear fins a flick with his finger to be sure they rotated freely. When a Sidewinder is launched, the missile's slipstream makes the disks rotate, providing inflight stability.

Next, he checked the four AMRAAMs hanging from the full-length pylons on either edge of the fuselage just below the conformal fuel tanks. Twelve feet long and seven inches in diameter, the radar-guided Advanced Medium Range Air to Air Missiles had the same deadly mission as the Sidewinders: destruction of other aircraft. The AMRAAM was a medium-range missile while the

59

ANTENNA · ELECTRONICS · INERTIAL REFERENCE UNIT · TARGET DETECTING DEVICE · ACTUATOR · BATTERIES/TRANSMITTER · ARMAMENT SECTION · ROCKET MOTOR · DATA LINK

Advanced Medium Range Air-to-Air Missile (AMRAAM) was a joint NATO development project led by Hughes Aircraft of the USA. After early teething problems, AMRAAM became a formidable fighting weapon.

60

Sidewinder was for employment closer in. He made sure the guidance fins were free to maneuver and that they were not damaged. He glanced upward toward the right wingroot and examined the opening for the M61A1 Vulcan 20mm Gatling Gun. It was loaded with 500 rounds of API—armor piercing incendiary—ammunition. The red banner on the breech safety pin hung down.

Tom made sure the LANTIRN pods, one under each engine just behind the intakes, were secure with heads undamaged. He then checked the AXQ-14 pod between them on the Eagle's belly. This pod would provide guidance to the AGMs as they blasted toward their target. He made sure the chaff and flare ejectors, located inside the belly just behind the LANTIRN pods, were also secure inside their four flush panels.

Then he performed the regular aircraft walkaround, looking for cuts on the tires, objects in the engine intakes, loose panels or missing panel fasteners. He checked the Jet Fuel Starter accumulator gauges at over 3,000 psi. He also made sure the tail hook, to be used in arrested landings if required, was snug against the fuselage, nestled between the two powerful engine afterburner sections. Finally, he checked that the afterburner "tail feathers"—the nozzle components—were all in place and connected to their actuator rods. "You're right," he said to Sergeant Collins. "She's ready to fly." Looking at the luminous dial on his "regulation-issue" dark metal wristwatch, Tom saw that it was precisely seven minutes before time to start engines. Over at the next parking space, he saw Pat Harris was already in the front cockpit, donning his helmet. He climbed the ladder. Dick Elton had already strapped himself into the rear cockpit. Tom strapped over the rail and settled into his seat. It felt good, as always. He savored the unique smell of the aircraft. Smells like a new car, he thought.

Sergeant Collins helped Tom strap on the aircraft. She removed the safety pins from behind the seat headrest and backed down the ladder. Briskly, she removed the ladder from the side of the aircraft and placed it flat on the ground, out of the way. Then she donned her headset and microphone, connected to the Eagle by a long cord leading to a terminal inside the nosewheel well. "Ready to start, sir," she said.

"Stand by, Jennifer," he directed. Pushing a fire extinguisher on wheels that was as big as she was, Sergeant Collins moved to the right of the aircraft, to the side and well forward of the engine intake. When the minute hand on his watch passed the 12 o'clock position, he reached down on the right console, raised the switch guards and flipped on the engine master switches. Then he reached forward to the right lower part of the instrument panel, in front of his right knee, and pulled the JFS T-Handle. He had made these motions thousands of times and could have performed them with his eyes closed.

"Starting Number Two."

Deep in the guts of the aircraft, the Jet Fuel Starter (really a small jet engine) whooshed to life and began its moan. When the pitch of the whine told him the JFS was up to speed, he cupped his left hand over the throttles and with his fingertips raised the finger lift on the front of the right throttle. The JFS whine decreased to a

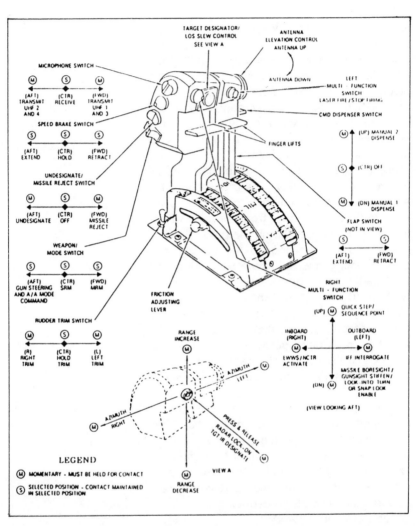

62

Fingers of pilot's left hand stay busy using the many controls on the throttle quadrant. By manipulating the buttons he controls communications and displays.

moan momentarily as it engaged and began to rotate the big Pratt and Whitney F100 engine. Ignition and fuel were provided automatically, and Tom, closely monitoring the engine LED panel, saw the engine light off at 18 percent engine RPM. He pushed the throttle forward into the operating range. The RPM continued to increase as the FTIT (Forward Turbine Inlet Temperature) climbed toward 680 degrees Centigrade and then fell back below 500. The RPM stabilized above 60 percent. Afterburner nozzles indicated full open.

Hydraulic and electrical systems, actuated by the engine's Airframe Mounted Accessory Drive (AMAD), signaled their presence with soft thumps and vibrations as they came on line, and both men checked as lights flashed on the instrument panel and consoles and indications on displays came alive.

The roar of air through the right intake, just forward of and below his right shoulder, was deadened by his tight-fitting headset and helmet. Sergeant Collins rolled her fire extinguisher to the left side of the nose. He could feel the smooth rotation of the powerful engine being transmitted to him through the airframe.

"Ready to start Number One," she said.

Tom pushed the fire loop test switch and saw fire lights come on for both engines. A female voice, "Fire" came through his headset. He released the test switch, tested the rest of the warning lights, and snapped on the UHF radio. "How do you read?" he asked Elton on intercom.

"Five square," Elton replied.

"How's it look from out there?" Tom asked the crew chief.

"Everything's normal-normal. No fluid leaks." He could feel the aircraft beneath and around him, almost like a living beast.

Tom flicked on his left and right Multipurpose Displays (MPDs) at the top of the instrument panel and the Multipurpose Colored Display (MPCD) in the lower center of the panel. He actuated the Head Up Display (HUD) in the windscreen and observed the symbology appear at eye level. Dick turned on two of each kind of

63

display in the rear cockpit. Tom took the Data Transfer Module from its slipcase in the lower zipper pocket of his G-suit and slipped it into the receptacle on the instrument panel.

He checked the fuel gauges for proper readings, pushed a button to check the hydraulic caution and low pressure lights, and said, "Starting Number One."

"Clear One," Jennifer replied.

Raising the fingerlift on the left throttle, Tom started that engine, checking all indications. When it was up to speed and the indications had settled down, the JFS automatically turned itself off. Its whine had long since been drowned out by the rush of air through the giant engines and the hot rumble of the engine gases. Johnson and Elton actuated the rest of the equipment, including the radar—Elton placed the inertial navigation system in "Standby"—and the navigation radios and the LANTIRN pods.

For a brief moment, Tom savored that unique feeling of power that always suffuses the cockpit after engine start. Feeling ready to fly, knowing the aircraft and he were about to take to the sky, raised and heightened his senses. As always, he felt as one with this big bird, which was now a part of his physical and mental being. From now until the flight was over, the Strike Eagle would be the medium through which he performed his mission. A miracle of modern electronics and hydraulics, she would respond to every command of his mind and will, transmitted to the aircraft through his talented hands. His eyes roved the familiar cockpit consoles, switches and displays. Everything was in the green. On his left-hand display, he called up the armament display, a plan view of the aircraft showing the armament stations, to be sure it correctly indicated what he was carrying on each station.

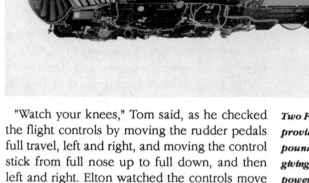

"Watch your knees," Tom said, as he checked the flight controls by moving the rudder pedals full travel, left and right, and moving the control stick from full nose up to full down, and then left and right. Elton watched the controls move in his cockpit. The crew chief insured that the flight control surfaces moved to the correct positions.

Johnson moved both intake ramp switches to normal and watched as the flat ramps at the top of each engine snapped to a partially-closed, downward position. This decreased the noise somewhat in the cockpit. With his right hand, he moved the canopy actuator switch to "Close," and the big canopy came down, sealing both cockpits in a realm of relative quiet. Engine bleed air now automatically began to heat the cockpit to the temperature Tom had selected. It was a welcome change from the raw air outside. "How's everything, Dick?"

"Inertial Nav aligned, everything else looking good," Elton replied.

"Thank you, sergeant," he said to the crew chief.

Two F100-PW-220 engines provide more than 27,000 pounds of thrust each, giving the F-15E controlled power in all regimes: slow flight near the stall, supersonic dash, air-to-air combat and long-range endurance.

65

"We are ready to taxi." For COMSEC (communications security) reasons, he did not contact the Command Post or check in with ground control in the tower, even though they were protected by HAVE QUICK. Even so, Elton would be flipping the UHF radio dial to the proper channels as they taxied from ramp to taxiway to runway.

Johnson actuated the LANTIRN navigation pod. As he looked through the wide-angle HUD, the night in front of the aircraft suddenly seemed to turn into day. He could clearly see, as if the darkness did not exist, everything in his field of view. Ramp, buildings and parked aircraft, in a slightly greenish tint, were as clear as in daylight. Looking left and right through the canopy, all was black outside.

"Good hunting," Collins said. Then she disappeared momentarily into the nosewheel well to disconnect her intercom cord. She reappeared at the left front of the aircraft, carrying the coiled cord, dragging two pairs of wooden chocks which had been blocking the wheels. She placed them on the side of the parking space, out of the way. Looking along the path Tom would taxi the aircraft along to be sure the way was clear, she raised her hands, clutching a small signal light in each above her head, and moved them backward and forward, signaling Johnson to taxi forward.

Tom moved the throttles forward slightly, and the powerful engines responded immediately. As soon as he felt the bird start to move, he retarded the throttles to idle and gently checked the brakes, his feet simultaneously pressing both rudder pedals. The nose dipped slightly in response. To his left, Sergeant Collins lowered her left arm to horizontal and Tom pressed the right rudder pedal, at the same time depressing the nosewheel steering button to the maneuvering position to get a sharper turning radius. Sergeant Collins popped him a sharp salute and he returned it with his gloved right hand.

"Everything looks good up here," he said. "You checked the route?"

Elton, with a hand controller on each side of his cockpit, was using the controller buttons and switches to call up displays on his MPDs and MPCDs.

"All the waypoints and HAVE QUICK frequencies are in the system," Dick said, "along with the attack check points and targets and their altitudes. The DTM staff has done its stuff. INS velocities are normal."

In front, Tom, using his own switches on the stick and throttle, was calling up displays and checking the HUD symbology.

Pat taxied behind him.

They turned 45 degrees left off the taxiway and rolled into the pre-takeoff check and arming area. Quick check crews checked the aircraft for leaking fluids, loose panels, cut tires and hot brakes. They were followed by the armorers, who swarmed under the aircraft, checked the security of all stores, removed preflight safety and arming pins and then withdrew. The two aircraft continued another 100 feet and stopped on the taxiway just short of the runway.

Tom looked at his watch. Almost 0700. After holding for a few minutes, he taxied onto the runway without a radio call, as pre-briefed. He lined the Eagle up with the runway, exactly straddling the white-painted centerline. With 20 seconds to go before brake release, he advanced the throttles smoothly to 80 percent RPM, firmly depressing the rudder pedals to hold the brakes. A higher power setting with the brakes set would cause the aircraft to start skidding.

He watched the engine exhaust nozzle indicators

67

move from nearly full to open to the minimum indication. FTIT temperatures moved into the 600s. Fuel and oil pressures were in the green. On the oxygen panel, the white indicator blinked each time he breathed. He could hear Elton's measured breathing as well. In the HUD, he looked straight down the runway. No obstructions. Scanning the panel, he saw that all instruments were normal. The Strike Eagle trembled slightly, eager to fly.

"Ready to go?" he asked quietly.

"Ready when you are," said Elton firmly. Tom released the brakes and immediately felt the bird surge forward. He advanced the throttles to the military power detent and watched the RPM on both engines stabilize at 94 percent. He watched the nozzle indicators move slightly toward open, as if they were expecting him to advance the throttle into the afterburner range. Each airman felt the big boot in his butt that came from the enormous thrust of the two big engines, even without using afterburner. They passed the acceleration checkspeed exactly as planned and in a few seconds were at rotation speed.

At 155 knots indicated airspeed, Tom eased the stick back, slightly aft of neutral. The nose came up. He made a slight stick adjustment to hold the aircraft altitude at 12 degrees nose up on the HUD. At 180 knots, exactly as planned, they left the ground. He immediately raised the gear and flaps, made the extremely short climb to 500 feet above the ground, leveled off and, as the airspeed climbed rapidly, reduced power substantially to hold their planned cruise of 400 knots. He rolled into a 45-degree banked turn around to their course heading, relying on the symbology in the HUD and the ability of the FLIR to "look" in the direction the aircraft was turning to avoid obstructions.

Multipurpose displays can be changed by pilot to show information he needs, when he needs it.

Glancing outside the cockpit, Tom saw complete darkness, pierced only by the lights of the town of Bitburg and other villages and towns along the way. Ahead, using the wide-angle HUD, he saw every detail of the terrain, including hills, roads, streams and obstacles.

"You seeing everything okay?" he asked. Elton

had the HUD picture on his right-hand MPD.

"All I need to," was the reply. There were a few seconds of silence as they enjoyed the feeling of the big bird loafing along at 400 knots in the velvet darkness.

Tom closely monitored the HUD, keeping the aircraft velocity vector inside the little box that gave him terrain-following information by moving up and down on the HUD, telling him when to pull up or descend to remain 500 feet above the rolling countryside beneath. The aircraft had an automatic terrain-following mode, but Tom, like most aggressive fighter pilots, liked to hand fly the bird most of the time. He could almost feel the Eagle's twin rudders carving tracks in the bottom of the low overcast just above them.

They flew northeastward toward their holding point. "Anything on the sensors?" Tom asked.

Elton scrutinized the integrated Tactical Electronic Warning System panel. The TEWS combined a radar warning receiver and active electronic systems. The systems could detect threats and, if the aircrew desired, automatically dispense flares or chaff, or both, to foil attacking missiles.

"Nothing but the usual air traffic control emissions," Dick replied. "If they're about to attack, they're showing remarkable radio and radar discipline."

They were on a discrete radio frequency, waiting for the execute signal, and heard no radio chatter at all. They cruised past the lights of Wiesbaden, the old resort city, crossing the Rhine, and tracked north of Frankfurt. They flew into their holding pattern over the Gedern TACAN right on schedule at 0716. It was pitch black below as they slowed to the holding speed, 300 knots. Tom flew a race track pattern with one-minute legs, making easy turns at 45 degrees of bank. The engines barely whispered.

The Attack

Jester One-One Takes Out a Bridge

The tension began to build. "Let's go over it again," Tom said. "After we leave this holding point, we'll go through the corridor. We'll pop up, pointing right at the target. You activate the radar and get a couple of good sweeps so you can identify the target and designate it. We'll use the inertial nav as a check. You put the radar in the Freeze mode. That will enable us to know where the target is in relation to our position at all times. We'll immediately descend, turn right, and fly down the ridgeline to the Initial Point. That'll take a little over five minutes.

"We reach the IP, turn left, radar activated again, and make the attack," Tom continued. "We stay at 200 feet above the mountains at 540 knots. Two minutes and 20 seconds to the target. We fly over the saddle seven miles out. We see the bridge on radar and in the HUD with the FLIR. I designate the bridge for the first weapon, on Station Two, and fire it. The AXQ-14 data link pod controls it and locks it onto the target. Five seconds later, you designate the target and launch the second bird, from Station Eight, and we start our turn away. I'll turn right. Okay?"

"Roger," said Elton, crisply. "Just be sure to keep us above those ridgelines, okay?"

They were near the end of the planned holding time when they heard the attack codeword. "Punchout, punchout, punchout!" a voice said on the discrete channel. No callsign, and no reply expected. Tom shoved the throttles forward and the Eagle leaped ahead. As the airspeed reached the planned 450 knots, they entered the overcast. Tom leveled off at 5,000 feet and watched the radar scan on his left-hand MPD. In short minutes, they were through the corridor and over enemy territory.

The TEWS came alive as fire control and SAM radars beneath them detected their presence and attempted lock-ons. "They know we're here now," Dick said. They listened for the dreaded chirp of High PRF, signaling a lock-on and SAM launch, but heard none. The adrenalin was flowing in both their bloodstreams now.

"They know where we've been," Tom said. "But they don't know where we're going." Their breathing on intercom was louder.

Tom thrust the stick forward to descend and rolled into a hard right turn to the southeast as Elton returned the radar to Freeze. They were quickly back on the deck, the left wingtip flirting with the jutting edge of a long mountain ridge that generally paralleled the Rhine, in safe territory miles away far to their right. They stayed at 450 knots, 200 feet above the crags. No groundfire or missiles yet, but they had been discovered.

"I'm setting up for the run," Tom said. He called up the Air to Ground format on his right MPD and selected Stations Two and Eight on the weapons display. The armament display showed that the weapons' caged gyros were starting up and their internal systems were activated. He

selected Arm, Nose and Tail, but the powered bombs would not actually be armed until he selected the Air to Ground Master Mode.

"Lots of fire control radar down the slope below us to our right," reported Dick. "So far, though, no air-to-air stuff."

"The Soviet air-to-ground aircraft are probably getting ready to launch in support of the ground forces in the Gap and the air-to-air jocks are looking for gaggles of F-15s and F-16s up high," Tom said. "They're not expecting us down here."

"Roger that," Elton replied. "Let's hope this surprise works. One good thing -- the defenses around the bridge won't see us until we cross the ridge line and pop out of that saddle." They were both outwardly calm, but they were breathing hard. Tom felt a tightness in his throat. Both men were determined to get the bridge, maybe get a MiG, and get out alive. The Eagle dashed along the rocky ridges, her systems responding to the demands of her masters.

"Five minutes and 15 seconds," Elton called.

"Rog. And here comes the tower," Johnson said.

In quieter times, F-15E of the 4th Tactical Fighter Wing is started and ready for takeoff.

73

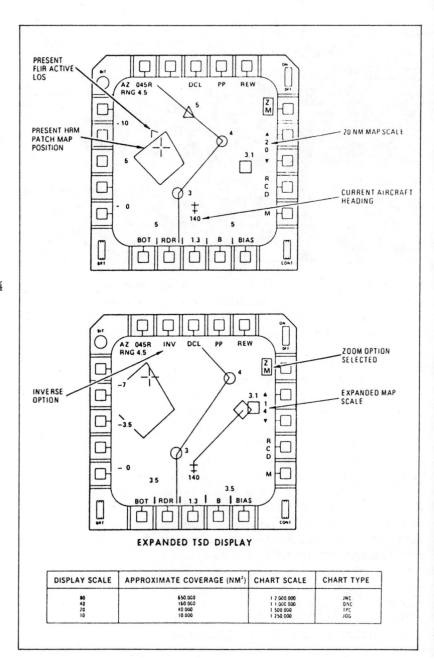

EXPANDED TSD DISPLAY

DISPLAY SCALE	APPROXIMATE COVERAGE (NM²)	CHART SCALE	CHART TYPE
80	650.000	1 2.000.000	JNC
40	160.000	1 1.000.000	ONC
20	40.000	1 500.000	TPC
10	10.000	1 250.000	JOG

74

He flipped the bird into a hard left climbing turn that caused their G-suits to tighten. The tower disappeared out the left side of the HUD. He shoved the throttles to full military power and watched the airspeed reading leap to 540. Attack airspeed! He then reduced power a bit to hold it.

Intently, he stared through the HUD, straining to see the rocks, crags and peaks flashing underneath the nose that only the FLIR could see. He watched the terrain-following box intently. Rocketing along at 200 feet at this speed, a split second late pull-up or an overreaction to a "Down" signal could mean disaster—the kind where they might suddenly find themselves in a black hole on a hillside with a smoke banner for a grave marker.

They approached the one minute mark—a minute and 20 seconds to go. Tom gripped the stick more tightly in his hand and checked that he had selected "Arm Nose and Tail" on the display, then actuated the Air-to-Ground Master Mode. "We're hot!" he said tensely.

"I'm picking up SAM sidelobe signals," Elton said in a calm voice. "On the nose. Part of the defenses for the bridge." He sat firmly in the back seat, one hand on each controller, watching his displays, actuating his switches and checking outside for visual cues. The control stick moved slightly between his knees as Tom smoothly controlled the aircraft. He had complete confidence in Johnson's ability—and luck—to get them in and out.

Tom pulled up to 4,000 feet (only 500 feet above the terrain at that point), which was 1,000 feet above the altitude of the bridge. He crisply rolled inverted to stop the climb and pointed the nose down in a 10 degree dive. They were flashing over the saddle, seven miles out. The

Moving map display gives aircrew members constant update on aircraft position and flight path ahead. Display can be zoomed or expanded, and radar picture or map chosen.

terrain gradually fell away beneath them to the gorge and the bridge. They slanted down toward the bridge, knowing the enemy below would soon be throwing up a barrier of flak. To the east, the sky was brightening as dawn tried to permeate the cloud cover. Below and ahead, green ZSU-23-4 tracers began to slash the blackness.

"I see it!" Tom called out. "Just like Falatchik's photo! I can see the river and the radio tower along the roadway to the left! I'm going to designate. And look! There are tanks moving across it right now."

Elton also could see the bridge on one of his displays. He scrutinized the tank profiles, long gun tubes jutting from turrets. They were moving

ZSU-X is a potent Soviet antiaircraft system, with tracked mobility and radar guidance.

single file, very close.

"T-90s! Just like Falatchik said," Elton added.

Using his second finger to move the Target Designator Control button on the right throttle, Tom slewed the aiming symbol over the center of the bridge and depressed it. The weapon system for Station Two was locked on. Glancing between the HUD and the display, he jockeyed the Eagle through a thicket of tracers toward the target. He watched the Range Caret move down the display from Maximum Range (RMax) toward RMin, waiting for it to reach the optimum (ROpt) position between the two.

The "Shoot" cue illuminated. Firmly, he thumbed the weapon release on the left top of the stick. There was a slight pause. He held his breath, listening to the stuttering sound of detonating anti-aircraft rounds trying to find the range and blow them from the sky. The Eagle was buffeted by the concussions of the explosions. Then there was the "clunk" of the weapon being explosively released from its station under the left wing, there was a loud searing sound, and the aircraft was bathed in the hot white light of the rocket motor plume as the bomb started its deadly flight.

"Your turn!" Tom said.

Dick Elton, using the switches on his left-hand controller, already had command of his weapon. The Shoot cue was already on and the Range Caret was moving toward RMin. He used the target designator control button to designate the target for his weapon, locked it on, and pressed another switch forward on the hand controller to launch the weapon. The firing sequence was repeated.

As soon as the second weapon launched, Johnson rolled into a 30 degree turn to the right and then rolled out. He wanted to keep the bridge in the field of view of the guidance pod. Elton

77

guided his weapon manually. They could see the white plumes of the weapon rocket motors, which rapidly became white points of light, as they thrust the weapons supersonically toward the target. A moment before impact, the rocket motors extinguished as the propellant was used up.

Then Tom's missile struck the junction point of arch and bridge decking and exploded in a huge gout of red and yellow flame. The bridge seemed to tremble. Ten seconds—an eternity—later, Dick's missile exploded just above the impact point of the first bomb. Their flight path, by design, took them over a ridge and momentarily screened them from the ground fire. Daylight was now firmly asserting itself, although it was still black in the shadowed valleys below.

Tom rolled smoothly left around the small mountain range that anchored the south end of the bridge. During the turn, they caught a glimpse of the carnage they had wrought. The center of the bridge and the arch both detached from the bridge on either side and fell in slow motion into the gorge. Before it struck the dark water in the river below, pieces of the giant structure from either side began to fall. Tanks on the bridge tumbled into the air like 40-ton toys. After realizing what had happened, a solid line of tanks began to bunch up on the road leading to the bridge, swiveling their long gun barrels like confused insects.

"Man, oh man," said Elton. "They're going to be sitting ducks for the ground attack birds coming in."

"Yeah," said Tom. "Too bad we can't stay around to watch. We've got to check out that MiG field to the north." The jagged terrain was flashing by, just under the belly of the bird, as he tried to use terrain masking for protection from missiles

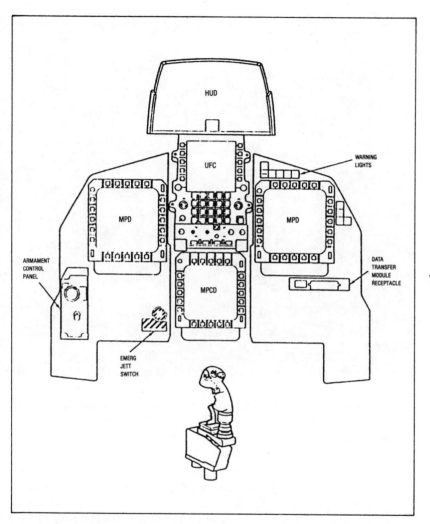

Pilot of F-15E has displays in his field of vision. HUD (Head Up Display) is a wide angle display showing vital flight data.

and ground fire. They were still drawing heavy anti-aircraft fire, but it was no longer tracking them very well.

"Wait a sec," Elton said. "We've got a SAM! Eight o'clock low. High PRF! They're launching!" Wordlessly, they watched as the SAM, pencil-thin, sharp-tipped, and as long as an F-15, streaked

80

SA-6 Gainful missile is for medium range air defense of Soviet divisions.

up out of the dark shadows, its light grey paint gleaming ominously in the weak daylight. It climbed to their altitude, then the nose lowered and it started to home in.

"Beam it!" Elton called hoarsely. Johnson was already turning to the left, slightly toward the SAM, to "beam it," that is, force it to make an attack at exactly a right angle to their flight path. This changed the doppler return the missile needed for its guidance system. Elton actuated the countermeasures system and a dense cloud of chaff was expelled from the Eagle's belly to confuse the SAM.

The SAM seemed to keep tracking them as they streaked northward. "Take her down! Take

her down!" Dick shouted. Johnson rolled the wings left past the vertical, stomped bottom rudder, and took them skimming down the mountain slope close beneath. They were supersonic. Neither man breathed. Suddenly, the missile veered off and exploded.

"The chaff worked," said Tom.

"So did our tactics," replied Elton. "It's good to know all this stuff we've been practicing all these years really works!"

"Yes," said Johnson. "And flying low, in this mountainous terrain, we gave its radar guidance system a lot of ground clutter to contend with, which helped." They streaked at full throttle up a valley, over a ridge line, and out of the bridge's

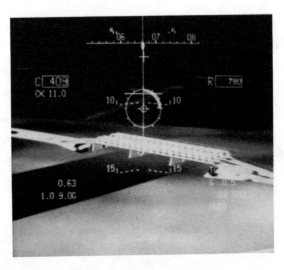

Infrared imagery changes night into day. In this peacetime shot, flight information from the HUD is superimposed on target bridge at night. Aircraft is flying on a heading of 066 degrees, 780 feet above the terrain.

defense area.

"Did we take any hits?" asked Johnson. Each man looked over the aircraft.

"Don't see any holes, and I didn't feel anything hit us," said Elton. "Guess we're okay."

"How far is it to that airfield, Haina?" asked Johnson.

"Couple of minutes," replied Elton.

"Rog. Let's set 'em up hot for guns and missiles! We're getting enough light for some eyeball to eyeball hassling!" Johnson said.

Still counting on the element of surprise, they headed north for Haina where the first of 12 MiG-25 Foxbats, armed for air-to-air combat, was just taking the number one position for takeoff.

First Blood

Round One with Gorshkov

Colonel Valerie Gorshkov led his squadron of MiG-25s to the single runway. Eleven Foxbats taxied in staggered trail behind him. Haina airfield was a small civilian field with one runway running generally east-west. During the recent series of exercises, Soviet engineers had lengthened and strengthened the runway to support jet fighters. The field lay north of the foothills of the mountain range where Johnson and Elton had knocked down the bridge. Situated on a narrow east-west plain, it was nestled in the lee of hills that formed the beginning of another mountain range to the north. Haina sat north of the autobahn running from Gotha to Eisenach, less than 30 miles from the Fulda Gap.

Gorshkov was old. He had been flying fighters for almost 30 years. In the late sixties, as a much younger man, he flew North Vietnamese MiG-21s against the Americans over Indochina. This war, he knew, would be his last, even if he survived it, and he was determined that Mother Russia would win. Like all Soviet pilots, he would gladly give his life for that purpose. But before he died, he wanted to fulfill a wish born in the skies over North Vietnam: to chalk up an American kill.

Today, Gorshkov and his pilots had been told, as the glorious war of liberation was beginning, they would join thousands of their comrades high over Europe, where they would battle thousands of NATO fighters with missiles and guns in an attempt to win air superiority. Gorshkov thought of the six AA-11 Archers under his wings. They were the most modern air-to-air missiles the Soviets possessed. They were equipped, like the American AMRAAM, with on-board terminal guidance systems. This meant that once he had designated the target for the missile, he could "launch and leave" it—the Archer would use its own on-board radar to home in on the target aircraft and kill it while he pursued other quarry. He did not know his first engagement was about to begin, not in the stratosphere, however, but just above ground level.

Hurtling north at 200 feet in the increasing daylight, the American crew tensely kept their bird low and fast. They flashed over towns, roads, rail lines, rivers and forests, and everywhere they saw the giant Soviet war machine on the move toward the Fulda Gap.

"Christalmighty! Have you ever seen so many trucks, tanks, and artillery pieces?" Elton ejaculated.

"And they're all carrying troops for the battle," Johnson responded. They were so low that they could see the Soviet soldiers raising their rifles to fire at them. But they were gone before many could draw a bead. Tensely, they watched, especially to the rear, for the rocket plumes of shoulder-mounted missile launches. They zigzagged east and west across their track, which was north toward Haina. The enemy air-defense net was activated now, and its emissions triggered indications on the TEWS display in Elton's cockpit.

MiG-25 interceptor held time-to-climb records for years. Sturdy and fast, it lacked agility and a look-down radar. When armed with the AA-11 Archer "launch and leave" missile it was a deadly foe.

85

Because they were traveling so low and fast, none of the enemy SAM sites had them in their horizon long enough to track, switch to high PRF, and launch.

"Probably their early warning and control Mainstay aircraft are getting some intermittent paints on us," Johnson said, "but we're so low that ground clutter must be screwing up their returns. They'll be taken out by dedicated mission aircraft pretty soon, and then we won't have to worry about them."

"Yeah, and changing direction makes it difficult for their ground spotters to predict where we're going," said Elton. "Climb a couple of hundred feet. The inertial says we're only twenty miles

Air-to-air weapons locations on F-15E airframe are for AIM-7 Sparrow, AIM-9 Sidewinder and AIM-120 AMRAAM.

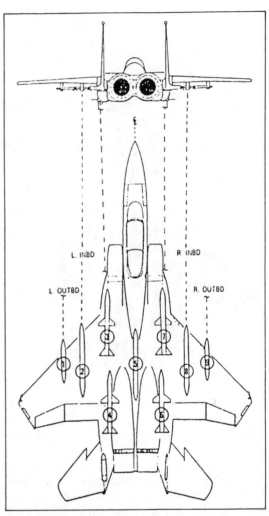

out. I need to get a couple of quick sweeps for a radar map."

Johnson broke hard left so the high resolution radar would have a 40-degree side cut on the airfield, popped the Eagle up for 20 seconds, slapped the bird down on the treetops, and broke hard right through a small valley. This was pretty country, he noticed. Farms, cows, probably pigs and chickens, too. All neatly laid out and fenced throughout the rolling countryside.

Elton had frozen the radar picture, and he now studied the radar map. Symbology showed him where the Eagle was in relation to the target. "Look," he said, "one runway with a parallel taxiway. Nothing on the parking ramp. But it looks like two, four, um, twelve contacts are on the taxiway. Oh, I get it; they're aircraft, taxiing out to take off right now."

"Well, let's get over there," said Johnson. "Maybe we'll get the leader as he comes off the ground." He rolled into a hard left turn and rolled out wings level when the inertial navigation system pointer was on the nose. He crosschecked the inertial as he observed a rail, highway and river junction that, he remembered, stood out on the map during their flight planning.

"You wouldn't shoot a guy in the back, would you?" Elton asked in mock astonishment.

"Hey, a kill is a kill, no matter where you hit the sumbitch," Johnson replied. He checked the armament control panel on the instrument panel by his left knee to be sure the Master Arm switch was still in "Arm." He flicked a glance at the HUD control panel at the top center of the instrument panel, just below eye level, and pressed the button marked "AA" to select the Air to Air master mode. The button illuminated. This told the Eagle's 256K central computer that they were now after aircraft, not ground targets. At the same time, Elton observed the AA advisory light on his left lower instrument panel illuminate.

When a Strike Eagle attacks, the computer gathers data from the aircraft sensors and uses it to compute steering, tracking and weapon launch parameters, which are translated into symbology on the HUD. The key element in this attack

87

sequence is the information provided by the Hughes APG-70 high-resolution radar in the nose, which the backseater operates to acquire and track the targets. He can acquire as many airborne targets as there are missiles aboard the aircraft, and the radar can provide pre-launch information, such as target location, speed, direction of travel and angle off, to the displays and missiles.

Using his thumb to actuate a three-position switch on the inboard side of the right throttle, Johnson selected "MRM" – medium range missiles. Johnson's armament display on one of his MPDs now showed a plan view of the Eagle, with "MRM" at stations 1, 2, 3, and 4. These were the four points on the edges of the fuselage just below the conformal fuel tanks on which were nestled the deadly AMRAAMs. When commanded by Johnson, station 1, front right, would launch first, followed, when commanded, by station 2, right rear, and then the two left stations. All also indicated "ARM" meaning each missile was in launch-ready mode.

The symbology in the HUD changed, too. The terrain-following box disappeared, replaced by the TD—target designator—box. If they got close enough to see the target aircraft—although, with AMRAAMs, they did not have to—it would appear in the TD box. When Elton or Johnson "locked up" the target, other symbology would also appear.

"The lead aircraft is halfway along his takeoff roll," Elton called, as he intently watched the radar scope, which he had now taken out of the freeze mode and put on "10 mile search." "He's taking off to the west." They were still a little too far out to actually see Gorshkov's aircraft with the naked eye (at a range of five miles, even a 747 airliner appears as only a dot on the windscreen).

Gorshkov was happy, as all fighter pilots are, to be leaving the ground for battle. But his smile changed to a frown as the tower excitedly called, "Air defense headquarters reports a bogey south of the field, eight miles out! A fast mover." A bogey! Could a NATO aircraft have penetrated the warning screen and be attacking him? He scanned the sky at his nine o'clock high, but saw nothing except the overcast. He pressed both throttles forward to be sure they were in full afterburner. He felt the brute force thrust of the engines accelerating his aircraft.

Then, of necessity, he brought his eyes back inside the cockpit to check airspeed and system pressures. Good. Everything in the green. He reached forward and flipped the gear handle up, waited a few seconds, and raised the flaps. As his airspeed started to build, he put his aircraft into a hard left turn toward his unseen adversary. He actuated his master arm switch and selected "missiles" on the armament panel. He searched the sky ahead, climbing toward the overcast. Nothing.

In the Eagle, Dick, his eyes glued to the radar display, used his thumb on the four-way button on his hand controller to slew the acquisition symbol over the little square dot that was Gorshkov. He depressed the button to effect a lock-on. Immediately, an aiming circle and a steering dot appeared on the display. At the top of the display, he read Gorshkov's speed at 350 knots and increasing. It also showed the Russian was pulling five Gs -- a hard turn. Another figure, the aspect angle, was increasing as Gorshkov turned more and more toward them. If he were pointed directly at them, the aspect angle would be 180. As Dick locked him up, it read 135L, meaning they were now at Gorshkov's ten o'clock position, moving toward eleven.

90

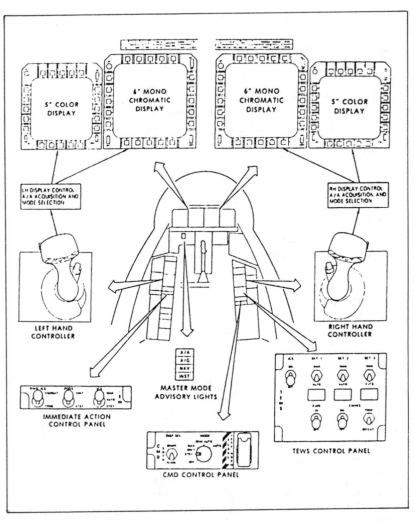

In the rear cockpit, air-to-air controls and displays can be manipulated and projected by either hand. WSO, coordinating with pilot, brings up displays.

The rate of closure of the two fighters was now more than 1,000 knots, and increasing. All this information was automatically relayed from the Eagle's sensors to the central computer. "He's turning into us and climbing above us," Dick called excitedly. "He's silhouetted against the sky. What a shot we've got!"

"Roger that!" Tom replied. "And his missiles can't see us because we're down here in the weeds with all this ground clutter."

They were in more than ground clutter. Enemy tracers and antiaircraft fire were increasing. In both airmen, the adrenalin was really pumping. All their senses were operating at top efficiency and everything appeared in amazing clarity. Ahead, the airfield defenses were coming alive. Red and green tracers were shooting up, even though the Eagle was still barely above the airfield's horizon line. The TEWS warned that SAMs were in the area, in search mode. On the airfield, Gorshkov's wingman was rolling on takeoff and number three was taking the runway.

Gorshkov was scanning the sky as well with his radar scope, eagerly looking for the bogey. He saw nothing because he was looking up and he had set his radar, as was customary on takeoff, angled slightly up. He knew the enemy aircraft was near because every gun in the area seemed to be filling the air with lead. He was beginning to feel that little flicker of dread that comes from not knowing the adversary's position. Like all fighter pilots, he knew that more than half the kills in the history of aerial combat have been scored when the target aircraft did not see the attacker and, in most cases, did not even know he was there. Even in training, there is no more uncomfortable feeling for a pilot than not knowing where the other guy is — he can kill you with his weapons, and you might even collide with him. Gorshkov cursed. Where is the bogey? He groaned, breathing hoarsely through gritted teeth.

Tom watched the radar display and HUD. He also saw the ASE circle growing larger in diameter and the aiming dot well inside the circle, meaning they were in the correct azimuth zone for a kill. All MRM positions on the armament display still

sequence and the rocket motor ignited to carry him, in his seat, up and out of the aircraft. He felt the roaring slipstream hit him like an icy claw. It pinned his arms back against the seat and drove his helmeted head back hard against the headrest. The seat tilted slightly head forward in its upward flight. He saw the flaming hulk as it sped beneath him start a steep dive for the ground. His parachute opened with a loud "snap" and he found himself descending safely to earth. It took a moment of comparative peacefulness before he became conscious of the continuing rattle of rifle and machine gun fire and the explosion of anti-aircraft shells tracking the speeding Eagle.

Tom rolled the bird back to the left in time to see the MiG, trailing a giant gout of orange and red flame and black smoke, start its final descent.

"Eee-ha!" Elton exulted. "Direct hit. One down, 11 to go!"

Gorshkov looked over his shoulder, toward the hot sound of the Eagle's engines, and saw the big bird streaking straight for the airfield. His wingman was off the ground and number

Early test of firing AMRAAM from F-15C at Eglin AFB, Florida, proving the aircraft-missile combination in live tests.

93

three was about to become airborne. Number four was at the spot where the narrow taxiway met the runway. Antiaircraft guns and automatic weapons were still firing, filling the air with dark smoke. Orange airbursts stood out in contrast to the dull grey of the overcast and the dark brown of the fields and foliage beneath him. Gorshkov landed, bruised, but miraculously, not seriously hurt, on a small hilltop.

As they closed in on the field, Dick said, "I've got two airborne on the scope. You going to go for them?"

"We can handle two," said Tom, "but I'm not sure we can handle 11. Why don't we try to stop this guy taking the runway? He'll bottle up the birds behind him. They'll have to turn around and taxi all the way to the other end of the runway. While they're doing that, we can get these two birds and head for home."

"Good plan," Elton agreed.

Tom flicked his thumb switch from MRM to GUN. The gun cross symbol appeared in the HUD. Tom took grim satisfaction in the thought

For heavy ground strafing, a 30mm gun pod was mounted on F-15E centerline. In production models, the 20mm M61A1 rapid firing gun is mounted internally at the right wing root.

94

of the 500 rounds of API in the ammunition storage drum, and of what the six-barreled M61A1 Gatling gun nestled in the right wing root would do with them. Firing at 6,000 rounds a minute, the gun produces almost a steady stream of lead.

They tore across the field at right angles to the runway. Tom lowered the nose slightly to get a bead on number four. At about a half-mile out, he moved the stick forward slightly to stop the aiming dot on the target aircraft and concentrate the burst. He depressed the trigger on the stick grip and felt the slight vibration of the gun firing. At 6,000 rounds a minute, the cartridges fire so rapidly that the gun emits a loud, continuous moan. In this case, it was the moan of death for Gorshkov's number four, who became the first Soviet fighter pilot to be killed in the war. The API rounds, each weighing almost half a pound, smashed into the fuselage, cockpit, fuel tanks and engines of the MiG-25 and caused it to erupt into a stationary, flaming, orange and red funeral pyre.

"Great shooting!" Elton exulted. "The dead bird is blocking the taxiway!"

They had been in ideal strafing range, between 3,000 feet and 2,500 feet from the target, for only a second. It was long enough to send 100 rounds into the target, killing it. Tom immediately brought the stick firmly back into his gut to raise the nose. He executed a five-G rolling pullout to avoid the ground and the exploding target. Elton and Johnson tensed their guts to help the G-suits fight the Gs.

"Let's find those other two birds before they find us," said Johnson. He flew north briefly to be over the sheltering terrain of the hills, making them a tough target for the MiG-25 radar. "I'm going to pull a hard 180 here and see if we can't pick them up. They were both turning south as they left the traffic pattern."

Johnson and Elton grunted loudly to help tense their guts against the Gs. Their G-suits clamped them in a comforting vise as the Eagle executed the turn, just above the crags below. Elton placed the radar in six-bar scan and intently observed the display.

Two-thirds of the way around the turn, Elton picked up two blips and said, "I've got a tally on two bogies at ten o'clock high, 10 miles. Looks like they're in combat formation." He depressed the button for a lock-on. "They're at 10,000, moving from our right to left, pulling four Gs at 450 knots. Go get 'em!"

On his hilltop, Gorshkov had watched the attack and felt a grudging admiration for the execution. He recognized the F-15E and realized all the intelligence reports about it were true. This, he mused, is a formidable all-purpose attack machine. Then his admiration turned to anger as he remembered what the American aircraft had done to him, almost before he had time to get his gear up.

Johnson, streaking on the deck for the two targets, did not see Gorshkov as he flew past the Russian on the hilltop. But Gorshkov got a good look at the aircraft and spotted the Deadly Jester harlequin mask painted on the side of the nose.

"We will meet again, Comrade," he said through gritted teeth. "And the next time, I will be the winner!"

Air to Air

More MiGs Taken Out

In the radar display, they watched the two aircraft above them in the overcast.

"They're turning, and number two is about 3,000 feet back of the leader on the outside of the turn," observed Johnson. The TEWS was going crazy, picking up SAM emissions from several directions, but no launches so far. Sporadic automatic weapons and rifle fire, mixed with the tracers of ZSU-23s, sprayed around them, but mostly behind them. He frowned slightly. They were attracting too much attention.

"Battle damage?" Johnson asked. Both airmen scanned the Eagle for hits, using their mirrors in the canopy bow to check six o'clock.

"We've got a couple holes in the left rudder," reported Elton.

"I don't feel any effect on our performance at all," replied Johnson. "Let's press on!"

Johnson's eyes narrowed as he scanned the symbology on the displays and the HUD. "We'll stay down here on the deck in the ground clutter," he said. He flew toward some rugged terrain that didn't look hospitable for vehicles. He flicked

98

MiG-25 Foxbat designers built for speed, not maneuverability; the aircraft was vulnerable in dogfighting and at low level. Two Tumansky turbojets generate more than 54,000 pounds of thrust.

the thumb switch from "GUN" to "MRM" and saw the AMRAAM symbology reappear on the display and in the HUD. He felt in complete synchronization with the Strike Eagle and, as a single entity, they moved in for the kill. Quickly, he surveyed the systems readings for signs of fuel, hydraulic or oil leaks and saw none.

"They're turning right into us!" Elton exclaimed, "and now they're descending. I'm picking up air-to-air radar emissions. Maybe they've seen us on their scopes and are going to launch their Archers!" Quickly, he slewed the designation symbol over the lead aircraft and locked on.

Johnson checked that the number two AMRAAM showed "Arm" on the display, and that the target was within launch range and azimuth. The shoot cues were flashing. He thumbed the firing button.

"Fox One," Johnson reported on intercom. The missile leaped off the rails, charged out ahead of the Eagle, and abruptly angled up into the overcast. Immediately, Elton locked up the other aircraft. Johnson repeated the procedures and launched his third AMRAAM.

This time, something went wrong. The missile sprang off the aircraft, but flew straight ahead and impacted on a ridge a mile in front of the speeding aircraft.

"Well, we'll never know what went wrong that time," Elton said tightly. "We were well within missile launch parameters." On the radar display, the first target aircraft suddenly showed a decrease in airspeed and began to descend very rapidly.

"We got him!" Dick said. "That's number three!"

"Only two of 'em were airborne," Johnson corrected him. "But no time to think about that," he quickly added. "The remaining MiG is inside minimum range for an AMRAAM and is continuing its descent. We're probably inside his RMin, too. What do you think he's going to do?"

Elton thought fast as Johnson rolled into a tight turn below the overcast. The MiG, still turning and descending in the clouds, passed directly over them, going in the opposite direction, and passed outside the limits of the Eagle's radar.

"Let's see," Dick said. "We knocked off lead, and then two and three took off while we strafed number four. Just like in our Air Force, three is probably the alternate lead and two is the least experienced guy in the flight. While we were turning around to find them, two and three joined up and three took the lead. We just shot down three. So this has to be two, who doesn't appear to know what he's doing. Otherwise, why is he coming down here through the overcast?"

99

"You're right," Johnson said. "He's inexperienced, or dumb, or both, and he wants to do this eyeball to eyeball. Hey—is that him just appearing on the side of the radar display?" He moved the throttles forward slightly, lighting the first afterburner stage and feeling the increase in thrust. He noted their airspeed moving up past 600 knots.

Elton locked onto the target. "He's doing 600 knots, turning hard toward us, and still descending. He should pop down out of the overcast any second. We're only two miles apart."

"There he is!" Johnson exclaimed. "Eleven o'clock slightly high. Is his radar on us?"

"Roger that," said Elton. "But we're in too close for his AA-11s. Look! He's fired one anyway!" Johnson tightened up the turn. They watched as the missile passed well off the left wing and exploded against a crag. "How you going to handle this guy? Gun?"

"I'll take a snap shot with the gun," Tom replied, "but there's no time to track on this pass." He moved the thumb switch to GUN and squeezed off a short burst. At the sight of his gun firing, the Soviet pilot abruptly broke right and zipped past the Eagle's left wingtip, about 500 feet out. Tom rolled hard left and turned across the MiG's track, behind him. The MiG pilot then rolled hard right, and the two aircraft came around head-to-head again. The Americans grunted hard under the press of seven Gs. The MiG pilot launched another missile outside of launch parameters and it did not track.

"This ... is ... crazy," Elton grunted. "We're ... unh ... roaring around ... here supersonic ... unh ... on the deck!"

"I'm gonna ... use the vertical plane ... and win the fight," Johnson grunted back.

Both aircraft reversed turn again, with Tom once again turning right across the MiG's track and behind it. As the MiG pilot rolled into his left turn, Tom was then at right angles to the MiG's flight path and at its six o'clock. He shoved the throttles into full afterburner and pulled the Strike Eagle into a sharp rolling climb, flying a classic barrel roll to get onto the MiG's tail. They punched up into the overcast as they were rolling inverted, and Tom stopped the roll to hold the inverted position, pulling the nose down through the horizontal plane as they descended out of the clouds into the clear air below. They were now directly above the MiG, watching it through the top of the canopy as it sped across the mountainous terrain. They were flying at a 20-degree angle across his flight path.

The MiG pilot had lost sight of his adversary. Tom performed a quarter roll so that the wings were now vertical and the aircraft was at the MiG's seven o'clock high. They were flying at over 700 knots. He jerked the throttles back out of afterburner range to cut speed. But they were almost abreast of the Soviet aircraft, too close to turn so that Tom could bring missiles or gun to bear.

"Keep turning left, you dumb Soviet bastard," Tom breathed. The MiG pilot, still looking for the Eagle, did just that! Tom eased in a little bottom rudder and moved the thumb switch to SRM. "I'm going to get him with a Sidewinder," he said. They descended smoothly into position behind the turning MiG.

"Great!" said Elton. "But hurry up, two SAM sites are tracking us."

Johnson watched the AIM-9 symbology in the HUD. He had an aiming circle and a steering dot, but because he was coming into position less than a mile behind the MiG he elected not to use the radar for tracking. The AIM-9 was a visual attack weapon, so Tom's job was to put

MiG-25 (far right) begins left turn parallel to Johnson's F-15E. Johnson rolls up and over, ending on MiG-25's tail (far left).

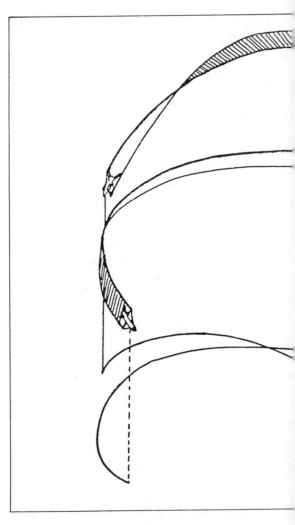

the target inside the aiming circle. He waited a split second for the missile seeker to "see" the target. The missile began to emit a tone. The aiming circle suddenly grew larger and in his headset he heard the steady tone emitted by the missile increase in pitch. The triangular Shoot Cue was visible in the HUD. The Shoot Cue and

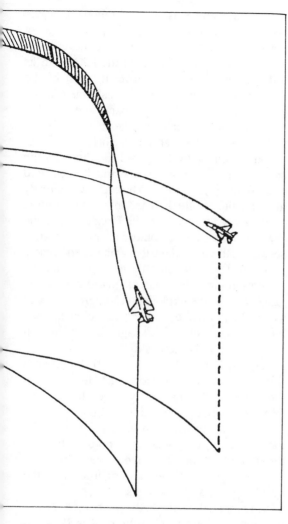

the shoot lights at the top of the windscreen began flashing.

"Shoot! Shoot!" Elton called. "One site is going to High PRF. They're going to launch a SAM!"

Tom firmly depressed the launch button on the stick twice. "Fox Two, Fox Two," he told Elton. The first Sidewinder flashed forward with a fiery hiss and was quickly followed by the second. Both missiles tracked directly to the hot tailpipes of the MiG. The Soviet pilot never knew what hit him. The aft end of the MiG, with its twin rudders, separated from the rest of the aircraft, which quickly was transformed into a flaming hulk. There was no parachute.

"Break left! Break left! Take it down!" Elton called tensely. "SAM at nine o'clock!"

Tom rolled the bird inverted and dived for the safety of the hilltops. Dick manually activated the jamming equipment. The SAM was already at their altitude, streaking in, only a few hundred yards away. A cloud of chaff popped out the bottom of the Eagle to confuse the missile's target seeker. At the same time, the jamming equipment succeeded in electronically fooling the missile by presenting a false target. Just out of lethal range, the missile exploded in an ugly black and yellow ball of flame. Some shrapnel nicked the left wing and belly of the Eagle, but the aircraft was not seriously damaged.

"Let's go home," Johnson said. "I think we've done enough for one morning." He looked at the clock on the instrument panel. It was only 0800 hours. But it seemed like High Noon.

Turning westward, Tom headed low level for the return corridor, which was north of the one through which they had entered East Germany. He jinked vigorously left and right to avoid the heavier patches of flakbursts.

Dick flipped the radio to the pre-briefed AWACS frequency. "Sentry Two-three, this is Jester One-One."

There was a pause. "Read you loud and clear, Jester One-One," came a firm voice from the big AWACS bird orbiting over Luxembourg. "This is Sentry Two-Three. Report."

"Scratch one bridge and a dozen T-90s," Elton

reported. "And chalk up three MiG-25s in the air and one on the ground. We're proceeding to home plate. Is the corridor quiet?"

"Our side of it is," reported the Sentry controller. "Good luck on what you have to go through on their side. Be alert for crashing aircraft. There's a roaring air battle going on at all altitudes above you." They could not see upward through the overcast to watch the scores of NATO and Pact aircraft engaged in deadly aerial conflict.

Below them, the two airmen saw an enormous ground battle underway. Tanks and artillery pieces seemed to be everywhere, firing rapidly. Trucks and armored personnel carriers pressed westward toward the Rhine. They were under attack by packs of F-16 Falcons, flying in flights of twos and fours. Close to the German border, NATO long-range artillery bursts and short-range conventional missiles impacted in the columns of tanks and trucks, stopping many in their tracks. There were flaming carcasses of aircraft on many hilltops, evidence of the air battle raging unseen above the overcast. As they watched, more

NATO AWACS aircraft, the E-3A Sentry, is a modified Boeing 707-720B aircraft. Circular radome houses rotating radar antenna; inside the aircraft is a powerful computer and communications complex for processing and conveying information for the ground and air battles.

fighters, mostly Warsaw Pact, fell from the skies. SAMs crisscrossed their flight path, some chasing after the F-16s supporting the ground battle. Anti-aircraft fire was being thrown up in all quadrants, and the flashes of near-miss airbursts reflected inside the cockpit like lightning in a thunderstorm. They flew west, zigzagging on the

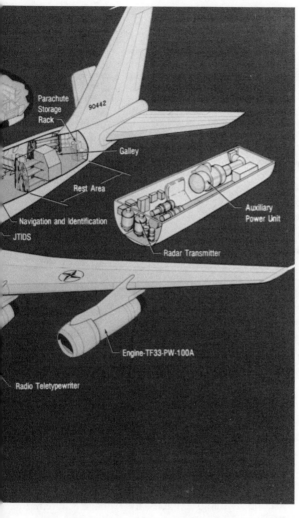

Internal layout of E-3A Sentry. Aircraft can stay aloft almost indefinitely, via aerial refueling, limited mainly by crew endurance.

Parachute Storage Rack

90442

Galley

Rest Area

Navigation and Identification

JTIDS

Auxiliary Power Unit

Radar Transmitter

Engine-TF33-PW-100A

Radio Teletypewriter

deck, supersonic. Then, north of Koblenz, they flashed across the Rhine and were suddenly over comparatively peaceful territory. Apparently, the NATO lines were holding for now.

"Check for battle damage again," Johnson ordered. Both airmen looked over the surfaces of the Eagle.

108

Mission controllers inside E-3A Sentry aircraft use multipurpose displays and expanded keyboards to manage the masses of information and communications channels on which they operate.

"Besides the holes in the rudder, I see a couple of holes in the outboard section of the right wing, and the decking on top of the left engine has some shallow slashes," Elton reported.

"Rog. Also some scratches on the canopy bow, just above the top mirror," Johnson responded. "Wonder when we picked those up? We're not leaking anything, so I guess the damage is minimal. We're lucky."

"And damned professional," Dick reminded him. "Shall we head for Bitburg?"

But what of Bitburg? Was the field still intact? Had its runways been destroyed? Should they land there, or head for the secret autobahn strip to the south, near Ramstein?

Land One
Strike Eagle

Returning for Repairs and a Few Stars

It was quiet inside the streaking Eagle. The men were still keyed up from the combat, and not yet home free. Their minds pushed away the combat scenes so they could concentrate on returning to base and whatever awaited.

"Call Sentry and ask for instructions," Johnson directed.

Dick keyed the radio. "Sentry Two-Three, Jester One-One. Say status of our home plate." The HAVE QUICK frequency hopping radio worked perfectly.

"Jester One-One. Home plate is intact. You are cleared to return to base."

"Rog. Jester One-One RTB."

"Let's make sure all armament switches are off or safe," Tom said. He went through the old ritual, starting on the aft end of the left console and moving his hands across the switches and buttons, across the instrument panel, the displays, and all the way around to the back of the right console, "Safing everything up."

Dick confirmed switches safe in his cockpit and also read aloud the armament safing checklist as he scrolled it down one of the displays.

Tom climbed to 5,000 feet, just under the thinning overcast, and turned southwest toward Bitburg. The battle zone was behind them. They had observed numerous fires and black smoke columns caused by Pact artillery and conventional missile impacts among the massed NATO ground forces they had passed over just west of the Rhine. But this part of West Germany still looked as it had in peacetime. The morning sunlight shone weakly through the overcast onto the farms, towns and villages in the lovely rolling countryside below. Here and there, a castle dominated the brow of a hill. In a few minutes, they were close enough to contact Bitburg approach control.

Elton dialed in the approach frequency and called. "Falcon approach, this is Jester One-One, 35 north east. Land one Strike Eagle."

"Jester One-One, Falcon approach. Switch to discrete frequency." Dick dialed the new frequency, which they had been given during the pre-takeoff briefing, and checked in.

"Prepare for radar approach to Runway 24," the approach controller instructed. "You will be sequenced with other aircraft landing and taking off. Be alert for numerous friendly aircraft in vicinity of the field. You will be notified on this frequency, if required, of enemy attackers. What is your state?"

Dick quickly noted the fuel gauge readings and computed their remaining flying time. He replied "One hour and 15 minutes."

"Roger. Turn to heading two-one-zero and descend to 2,500 feet."

Tom rolled into a 45-degree bank to the left and rolled out wings level when the heading indicator showed 210 degrees. Both the INS and the TACAN indicator showed Bitburg to be at one o'clock, moving toward two. He retarded

the throttles to 75 percent and began a gradual descent to 2,500 feet. The airspeed slowed to 300 knots and the roar of the slipstream diminished.

"Falcon approach," Tom called, "be aware Jester One-One has sustained minor battle damage. But this is not an emergency."

"Roger, One-One. We'll have crash equipment standing by as a precaution."

As the INS and TACAN indicators moved to 240 degrees, the approach controller instructed, "Jester One-One, turn to two-four-zero degrees. Switch to final approach frequency."

As Dick changed to the new frequency, Tom popped the speedbrakes and smoothly turned to the new heading. As the airspeed dropped to

F-15E above the clouds, a rare appearance in daylight and clear weather.

250, he lowered the flaps and landing gear. They were eight miles out, with the field in sight on the nose. The approach symbology was in the HUD. There were more than a dozen aircraft in the approach and departure patterns, pilots twisting their heads from side to side to remain clear of each other and following instructions from the controllers.

"Jester One-One, this is your final controller. How do you read?"

"One-One, five square," Tom replied.

"Roger, do not acknowledge further transmissions." Tom slowed the aircraft to 160 knots and started his descent when directed by the final controller. The cockpit became almost unnaturally quiet as the sound of the slipstream turned to a whisper. Once again, since each airman had set his oxygen system to 100 percent, the sound of their breathing was audible on the open mike of the intercom.

Tom set the throttles to hold the airspeed, making minute power adjustments to stay glued onto the glideslope. In the HUD, he held the velocity vector on the crossed hairlines of the

At Bitburg, pilot of the
112   *36th Tactical Fighter Wing wearing protective clothing checks maintenance records of his F-15C. F-15C and D models of the 36th flew and fought the air superiority daylight fight.*

glideslope and azimuth indicators. The angle of attack indicator stayed steady all the way down to touchdown. Another squeaker and puffs of blue smoke. Another Johnson smile. The waiting red fire engines, their motor exhausts roaring, raced down the side of the runway, pacing the big Strike Eagle after Tom lowered the nose at 80 knots and then slowed to turn off the runway.

Looking over the airfield during the rollout, they could see most of the F-15s that had been in the shelters and on the parking ramp in the predawn darkness were gone.

"Looks like most of the wing is off fighting the war," Johnson said. "I wonder why the other side hasn't attacked here yet?"

"Maybe our side screwed up their strategy," Elton said. They stopped briefly while the after-landing crew scurried under the bird to install the landing gear downlock safety pins and the armorers safed up the remaining missiles. Then they taxied back to their original parking spot. They turned off all the radios and electronic equipment as they maneuvered into the parking spot, directed by Sergeant Collins. Elton turned off the INS after they came to a stop, having recorded the system's vector velocities.

Tom flipped the intake ramp switches. The flat plates topping the air intakes snapped up on both sides of the cockpit. He actuated the canopy handle and the big shiny canopy, hinged to the fuselage behind Elton's seat, silently raised above both cockpits.

Johnson stopcocked both throttles and the engines died. In the silence, the crew chief placed the ladder over the canopy rail and climbed up to the cockpit. As she replaced the safing pins in the front seat headrest, the airmen removed their helmets and enjoyed the feeling of the cool morning air on their damp hair. Both men were

114 *Technician services the APG-70 radar, accessible at eye height, to prepare aircraft for next mission.*

drained, physically and mentally.

"What have you done to my bird, sir?" Sergeant Collins asked, her eyes widening as she saw the battle damage on the left wing, the rudder, and the top of the fuselage.

"Nothing a little sheet metal work won't fix, Jennifer," Tom said. "Basically, this bird is fine. We bumped into some unfriendly people on the other side and this was their way of objecting to our presence. This baby can really take it, and she brought us home okay.

"You can be really proud of your bird today. We knocked down a bridge, shot down three MiGs and blew up another one on the ground. And we still had some missiles left."

Chief Master Sergeant Knight, the grizzled line chief, smartly turned out in his pressed fatigues and field jacket, walked to the foot of the ladder. "Colonel Crawford is on the way out in his car, sir. He radioed that he wants to talk to you."

"Did you hear, Chief?" Sergeant Collins interjected. "We knocked down a bridge and got four MiGs!"

"Did we, now?" Chief Knight queried with a

smile. He remembered back to the Southeast Asia war. He was a buck sergeant back then, an F-4 crew chief in the Wolfpack wing in Thailand. He had felt that every MiG his Phantom shot down belonged to him as well as the aircrew. "Congratulations. Well, go get the paint. One star for each MiG. On the left side of the nose. And tell Sheet Metal to get somebody out here to repair these holes. I'm sure this bird will fly again tonight."

Sergeant Collins moved off smartly to get the paint.

"That's only three stars, Chief," Tom corrected. "One of the MiGs was still on the ground."

Colonel Crawford arrived. Now relaxed and

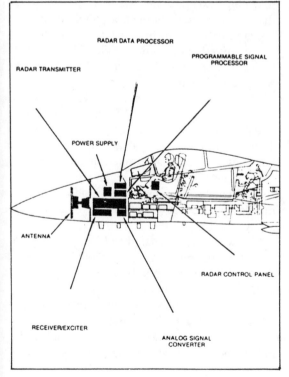

Block diagram of major components of APG-70 radar in the F-15.

115

RADAR DATA PROCESSOR

PROGRAMMABLE SIGNAL PROCESSOR

RADAR TRANSMITTER

POWER SUPPLY

ANTENNA

RADAR CONTROL PANEL

RECEIVER/EXCITER

ANALOG SIGNAL CONVERTER

revived, the two airmen unfastened their leads and safety equipment and descended to the ramp. Colonel Crawford got out of his car to congratulate them. He had followed their flight in the command post and had heard Sentry Two-Three's after-action report radioed to CINCUSAFE.

They got into the blue sedan and Colonel Crawford drove them to the maintenance debriefing shack (actually, a large house trailer), where they sat down at one of the small tables, filled out the maintenance sections on the Form 781A and gave the debriefing technicians an oral report of the aircraft's performance.

Then they walked next door to the intelligence section. Both Tom and Dick slapped Falatchik on the back. "It was just like you said," Johnson told him, "except there was more SAM activity than we expected. Nothing a couple of Jesters couldn't handle, you understand. At least, not when we're flying a Strike Eagle." They related their experiences on the mission. Chick beamed. Now he felt a part of the Jester team.

When the debriefings were over, Crawford invited them into his office for a cup of coffee. "We'll talk about your next mission," he promised. They sat down in the sparsely furnished room. On Crawford's standard Government issue desk were an F-15 model mounted on a pedestal and a single family photo: himself, his wife— a pretty, middle-aged woman—and two college-age youths, a boy and a girl.

"My wife was evacuated to England with the rest of the dependents a couple of weeks ago," the Colonel said. "The kids are in college in the States. My son's a senior at Purdue. Engineering major. He'll be commissioned out of AFROTC when he graduates." He paused. "Wants to be a fighter pilot, like his Dad," he added, with pride in his voice. "What about your families?"

"They're at Bentwaters," Elton said. "Two of mine are in middle school and one is in high school."

"My two boys are in high school," Johnson added. "The oldest will graduate next June. Wants to go to the Air Force Academy."

"Hopefully, this will be over by then," Colonel Crawford replied, bringing their thoughts back to the war.

"How about a situation report, sir?" Johnson asked. "Why haven't we seen any Soviet damage beyond the battle area near the Rhine? We were pretty sure they'd hit fields like Bitburg first and that we'd be operating out of bare bases in Germany or our big bases in England by now."

"There's plenty of activity out of our bases in England," Colonel Crawford replied. " F-111s and Wild Weasels are escorting F-16 strike packages and F-15Es are hitting high-value targets in the Soviet rear. The reason the Pact hasn't been able to hit bases like Bitburg is that we got a head start on them. As you crossed the border this morning, F-117 Goblins leaped off. They blew the Soviet Mainstays out of the sky before they knew what was happening. Big silence upstairs.

"Since about 0715, the Pact attack birds have had no on-scene direction," Crawford continued. "They took off in huge waves and could not contact their airborne flight directors. Of course, they didn't know at first that the Mainstays had been shot down. So, while they were milling around, our AWACS aircraft began directing hundreds of our F-15s, Tornados and Harriers in coordinated, concentrated attack waves against them. We've had Weasels, Tornados and F-16s flying flak and SAM suppression, and it's working. Don't misunderstand. It's been expensive. We've lost dozens of aircraft, but the other side has lost hundreds."

"Then we're on the offensive!" Johnson chuckled.

"For the time being, although the politicians might not say so," Colonel Crawford said. "But don't forget, our birds will be returning to refuel soon. We could be hit while we're turning them around. I'm sure we've got birds in reserve for protection during the turn, but the other side probably has reserves, too. They'll be here soon enough."

Crawford sipped his coffee. He sat the cup down, spun his chair to the left, and bent over his safe. He dialed the combination on the Sargent & Greenleaf lock, swung the door open, and pulled out a folder. Its cover was emblazoned with the TOP SECRET legend in letters three inches high. He slapped the folder on the desk and beckoned Johnson and Elton to come closer. Crawford opened the cover and removed a marked aeronautical chart and several aerial photos.

"Now, about your next mission," he said. "You're going to knock out a very important train."

A New Target

Aiming for a Key Soviet Command Center

was still furious. Having been shot down almost
before he had wheels in the well, he had been
picked up by a Hind helicopter and delivered
back to the airfield.

There, firefighting crews were finishing up the
job of extinguishing the burning remains of the
other MiG-25, the one that Johnson had caught
on the ground. Gorshkov took command of the
operation to work off his frustration. He supervised
the large tracked crane that lifted the hulk off
the taxiway, making the runway accessible from
either end.

Only then did he head for the intelligence tent,
where he reported the insignia he had seen on
the nose of the Strike Eagle that had destroyed
four of his aircraft and almost killed him. "It was
an American F-15, and the symbol was a theatrical
mask, laughing, with a comet or meteor flying
near it," he said.

The intelligence officer operated his field
computer. He called up, one by one, the known
hundred-odd U.S. Air Force unit insignias on the

CRT. After a short search, he said, "Is this it?"

Gorshkov looked at the image on the tube. "Yes," he said vehemently. "That's what the bastard had painted on the side of his aircraft."

"The 461st Tactical Fighter Squadron," the intelligence officer read from the text. "Nicknamed 'The Deadly Jesters.' Oh, look at this. That squadron is stationed in England. What was one of its aircraft doing here so early this morning? Our intelligence says none of those aircraft have been forward deployed. They are still carried at Bentwaters. Did NATO have intelligence that we were attacking this morning? Have they reinforced already? Better report this to headquarters." He tapped the computer keys and filed the electronic report.

"The 461st, eh?" said Gorshkov. "The Deadly Jesters? Jesters. We will see who has the last laugh the next time." He left the intell tent and strode toward his own squadron area.

At that moment, the Western TVD Command Train was rolling from its secret railyard base toward its forward command position. On the train, Red Army Gen. Mikhail Kalishni, Supreme Commander of Western Forces, anticipated the coming battle. He buttoned his tunic and, glancing in the mirror, used a finger to smooth his bushy, graying mustache. Then, with a confident step, he entered the first command center car, located just behind his personal car.

The duty officer briefed him. "Apparently, the NATO forces were expecting our attack. We have suffered known losses of 250 T-90 tanks and 300 armored personnel carriers. NATO long-range artillery, short-range conventional missiles, and attack aircraft have been hitting us since we launched the attack at dawn. Their attack helicopters have been taking a heavy personnel toll on the battlefields. Casualties suffered from all enemy

Deadly 20-pound SA-7 missile is carried and launched by one man. Air guards on the Western TVD train used SA-7s. Its infrared homer seeks aircraft engine exhaust out to six miles range.

attackers are estimated at 10,000 Soviet soldiers killed or wounded."

"What are we doing to them?" Kalishni asked. "What about our attack across the FEBA?"

"The ground attack was launched, but close air support and interceptor aircraft have been uncoordinated and, so far, ineffective. Somehow, they have knocked down all of our airborne control aircraft, and we have been unable to establish effective command and control. Your Air Component Commander, in the next car, is directing the air battle."

"What about air losses?"

"We have had 400 fighters and attack aircraft shot down," the officer shot back. "They have lost 60 and are starting to return to their bases to refuel and rearm. Our fighters are doing the same. Their ground forces have lost 250 tanks and 140 armored personnel carriers. We estimate their personnel losses at around 6,000."

"What about the surprise flank attack?" Kalishni queried.

"A key bridge was destroyed by a lone attacking

aircraft about an hour ago. The tanks that were to have supported the thrust into the NATO right flank have been bottled up," he answered.

"How long to repair the bridge?" Kalishni asked.

"Too long," said the briefing officer. "Days. It bridged a deep, wide gorge. Your subordinate commanders have already given the order for the supporting tanks to proceed north around the mountains to the main autobahn leading toward the Fulda area. They will be in position to support the attack tomorrow." He was suddenly handed a sheet of paper torn by a sergeant from a dot matrix printer.

"More bad news," the briefing officer said. "The supporting tanks are now under attack by scores of NATO air-to-ground fighters supported by electronic warfare aircraft. Losses are unknown."

Kalishni strode angrily into the next command car. The train was now approaching Leipzig over slowly rising terrain. They rolled west-northwest through Leipzig and out again into the countryside, which began to become more rolling and picturesque. The route became more easterly.

Another 20 miles westward, and they passed the small town of Halle-Neustadt. Then the tracks left the main line. They now led northwestward. The train rolled another 30 miles and passed Eisleben, a small town on the edge of low forested mountains, about 30 miles east of Halle-Neustadt. At Eisleben, it turned southwest. Twenty miles farther west they encountered a large village named Sangerhausen, and there the tracks forked. The train took the westbound line. It headed for Nordhausen, but 19 miles past Sangerhausen, the train came to a jerking halt with squealing airbrakes.

"We are at the spur, Comrade General," a colonel told Kalishni. Kalishni moved to the door of the car, lowered the window, and leaned out.

Looking back, he could see the train had rolled

past the junction with a spur line that ran northeastward into the mountains they had been skirting. As he watched, one of the train crewmen hopped down off the back of the train and threw a switch. He jumped back onto a short ladder fastened to the end of the last car and signaled with a hand wave to the engineer. The train rolled slowly backward, curving to the northeast along the spur.

"This spur was built to serve an iron mine back in the mountains," the colonel said. "It was closed a couple of years ago, but the track is in good condition." They rolled slowly along the tracks, moving through a valley that was wide at first, but gradually narrowed. A small stream bubbled in its deep course alongside the tracks, which followed its banks. After about 10 miles, the valley suddenly narrowed to only 500 yards, forming an entrance to another, much smaller valley. When they passed through the narrow entrance, Kalishni saw that the valley widened out again somewhat, but it was only a half-mile wide and about six miles long. The tracks and

SA-9 Gaskin missiles on wheeled carriers in Moscow parade. SA-9s protected Haina airfield.

123

stream hugged the eastern wall of the valley.

This was their final secret operating location. The valley was oriented exactly north-south, the tracks ending at the old mine in the north end. In the States, the valley would have been called a box canyon.

Kalishni liked the location. "We will not be found here," he said confidently.

The train could only be spotted visually from almost directly above, because the steep canyon walls extended upward on both sides and to the rear of the train for almost a thousand feet. Only at the narrow canyon entrance could the train be seen from a low angle, and only through the narrow opening. Even then, all that could be seen was a frontal silhouette of the engine far up the valley. The general deployed his SAMs on the heights above the valley, where they would have good coverage in all directions. Half of his anti-aircraft guns he deployed in camouflaged positions on the valley floor, and half he kept on the train. Two dish antennae were sited on the tops of nearby hills for burst data transmissions. They aimed upward at a geostationary satellite far out in space used for communications with Moscow. Other antennae on the train and in the surrounding wooded hills were for interface with different satellites and with ground stations of his subordinate commands. By late afternoon, Kalishni's headquarters was in full operation. He was in firm control, directing the battle, and he was confident his train was safe from detection or, if detected, well protected and able to beat off any air attack.

Mapping It Out

Mavericks Will Do the Job

Back at Bitburg, dozens of F-15s, including the three other Jester F-15s, had landed, refueled, rearmed and returned to the battle before the inevitable Soviet air attack came at 1600 hours. Eight Su-24 Fencer aircraft attacked with air-to-ground missiles and iron bombs. They were escorted by 12 Su-27 Flanker-B fighters. With their pulse doppler radar, high thrust-to-weight ratio and a full complement of air-to-air missiles with on-board terminal guidance, the Flankers were almost a match for the defending F-15s.

The attackers were met as soon as they crossed the Rhine, and tenaciously opposed by 10 F-15 Eagles all the way to Bitburg and then all the way back to Soviet territory. After five minutes of bombing and a spectacular low-level air battle that culminated right over the base, the attacking force was driven off.

Sergeant Collins and other people on the base watched from the tenuous safety of bunker entrances as aircraft and missiles streaked across the sky above them. "Look," she said, as an F-15 launched a Sidewinder right up the tailpipe of a

fleeing Flanker, "that's a Jester!" The killer Strike Eagle crew happened to be Pat Harris and Mike Gurth, who were returning from a ground attack mission.

The onlookers saw aircraft on both sides take hits, some bursting into flames, others trying to withdraw and being pursued from the fight. Sometimes a parachute deployed, holding out hope for a survivor. Throughout the battle, the air was filled with the constantly changing pitch of roaring engines as the fighters maneuvered for position. The heavy crump of bombs and the sharper crack of air-to-ground missile warheads exploding on the base was deafening. The hot odor of cordite also permeated the atmosphere,

Su-24 Fencer is a swing-wing attack aircraft similar to, but smaller than, the USAF F-111. Pilot and weapons system officer sit side-by-side in the cockpit. Ordnance load carried externally is more than 17,000 pounds.

127

and black smoke plumes ascended from the flaming pyres of crashed aircraft and burning buildings.

The attackers lost six Fencers and eight Flankers, but not before they had cratered the Bitburg runway in three places and destroyed three F-15s being rearmed on the ramp. Four defenders were shot down. The moment the attack ended and the air battle moved away, Sergeant Collins and the other crew chiefs sprinted from their shelters to help fight the fires burning on the ramp and in the hangar area.

"We going to be able to get off tonight?" Johnson asked that night as he and Elton took their places in Falatchik's briefing room. "We need to hit that command train before it can become effective in directing the Soviet forces."

"No sweat," said Colonel Crawford. "You'll be using the ALARS." The Alternate Launch and Recovery System, a 6,000-foot camouflaged runway equipped with mobile arresting gear, had been constructed at Bitburg two years earlier. It was on the perimeter of the base and oriented in the same direction as the main runway.

"The Rapid Runway Repair teams will have the main runway back in commission well before dawn," Crawford continued. "You don't really need a long runway, though, with the engine power you have available."

"Right," said Elton, "and our ordnance load is

128

relatively light. Mavericks are perfect for this mission."

They would be employing reliable Maverick AGM-65 Imaging Infrared missiles. Eight feet long and a foot in diameter, each Maverick weighed 485 pounds, including the 125-pound shaped charge warhead. In flight, keying on the heat emissions from the target, Elton or Johnson would designate the target for each missile, lock it on and launch it, letting the missile follow its course to destroy the target. It was a "launch and leave" weapon, which enabled the crew to turn away before reaching heavy close-in target defenses. With this type of missile, they also did not have to wait for it to hit the target before launching

F-15C of the wing commander of 36th TFW at Bitburg in more peaceful times. Su-24 attackers cratered the main runway at Bitburg, forcing operations onto the alternate landing and recovery system (ALARS) strip. Aircraft were prepared to operate from emergency strips on the German autobahn system.

129

additional birds.

The F-15 could carry six Mavericks, three under each wing. If given the opportunity, the crew could hit six targets in rapid succession on the same pass.

Falatchik began his briefing, using map and viewing screen. "We know the Western TVD Command Train left Dresden early this morning en route to its strategic war fighting location. The TVD commander and his battle staff are aboard." He was using his pointer to delineate the right of way of the main east-west railroad in East Germany.

"By tracking its radio emissions, and by comparing ELINT information with reports from agents, EUCOM followed it through Leipzig, Halle-Neustadt, Eisleben and Sangerhausen. The train never passed the next town on the main line, Nordhausen, so we know it is holed up somewhere in this area, on the southern edge of the Harz Mountains." He pointed to the rail line as it skirted the edge of forested mountains.

"You mean you don't know exactly where it is?" asked Johnson.

"Its emissions have been pretty sparse for most of the day," Falatchik replied, "so we don't have an exact location yet. But the one logical place it could be is this spur"—he pointed to it on the map—"leading to an old mine. It's the only place they could turn off the main line to hide. See how the spur leads into this little box canyon? It would be a perfect place to hide the train and it would be well protected by the walls of the canyon. This whole area is heavily forested."

The Jesters studied the map closely. "What about defenses?" Elton asked.

"There have been none reported in that area so far," Falatchik responded. "But the command train has its own AS-11 SAMs, the latest model, and plenty of anti-aircraft protection."

"Then we shouldn't have to worry about getting hit until we get there, right?" Johnson gibed.

Falatchik didn't fall into the trap. "You'll be flying over and through everything the Pact's got all the way to the target and all the way back, so I wouldn't say it's going to be a piece of cake."

Johnson and Elton smiled wryly.

"Your entry corridor will be available at 0500 through here," Falatchik continued, pointing to an area east of Bad Hersfeld, "and your exit corridor will be open 50 minutes later here." He pointed to an area just east of Kassel. They would be coming out north of where they entered enemy territory.

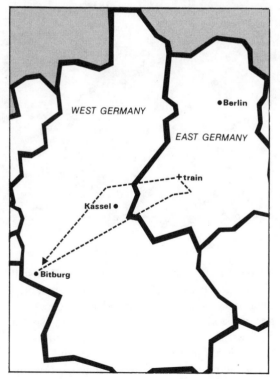

For their second mission, the Jesters penetrated more deeply into East Germany, to a concealed rail siding on the southern edge of the Harz Mountains.

132

Prototype Strike Eagle F-15 on static display, demonstrating extraordinary variety of bombs, rockets and missiles it carries.

Falatchik finished his briefing with the usual escape and evasion (E & E) and other essential information, listing the command radio frequencies and mission call signs. They were to transmit a codeword, "Smashup," three times in rapid succession if they knocked out the train.

The two airmen left the intelligence briefing

room and entered one of the operations planning rooms. Elton selected and unfolded a TPC E-2C Tactical Pilotage Chart. The scale was 1:500,000. There was plenty of terrain feature detail. Laying it flat on a planning table and using the edge of a mission plotter to smooth out some of the folding creases, Dick studied the target area

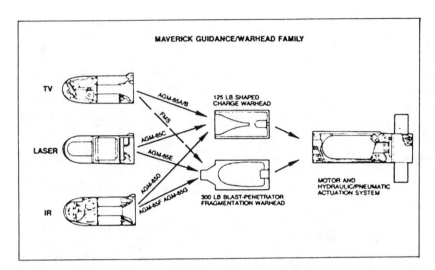

MAVERICK GUIDANCE/WARHEAD FAMILY

TV — AGM-65A/B

LASER — FMS, AGM-65C, AGM-65E

IR — AGM-65D, AGM-65F AGM-65G

125 LB SHAPED CHARGE WARHEAD

300 LB BLAST-PENETRATOR FRAGMENTATION WARHEAD

MOTOR AND HYDRAULIC/PNEUMATIC ACTUATION SYSTEM

134

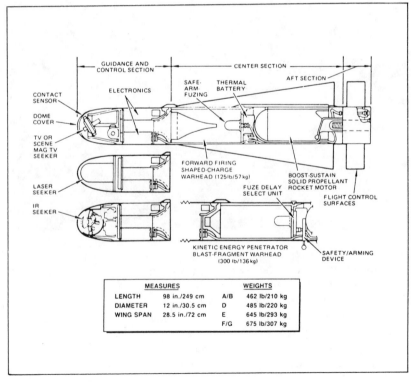

GUIDANCE AND CONTROL SECTION — CENTER SECTION — AFT SECTION

CONTACT SENSOR
DOME COVER
TV OR SCENE MAG TV SEEKER
LASER SEEKER
IR SEEKER

ELECTRONICS
SAFE-ARM-FUZING
THERMAL BATTERY

FORWARD FIRING SHAPED-CHARGE WARHEAD (125 lb/57 kg)
FUZE DELAY SELECT UNIT
KINETIC ENERGY PENETRATOR BLAST-FRAGMENT WARHEAD (300 lb/136 kg)

BOOST-SUSTAIN SOLID PROPELLANT ROCKET MOTOR
FLIGHT CONTROL SURFACES
SAFETY/ARMING DEVICE

MEASURES		WEIGHTS	
LENGTH	98 in./249 cm	A/B	462 lb/210 kg
DIAMETER	12 in./30.5 cm	D	485 lb/220 kg
WING SPAN	28.5 in./72 cm	E	645 lb/293 kg
		F/G	675 lb/307 kg

intently and used a pair of dividers to measure distances.

"Look. Here's where the spur breaks off from the main line," he said. "It runs northwest for about 10 miles through this rising terrain. Actually, it seems to follow the banks of a stream coming out of the mountains. There's heavy forest cover all along the way."

"Yeah," Johnson agreed. "And here," he pointed with a pencil, "the rail line goes into this smaller valley. Look how close these contour lines are. Pretty steep sides on it. The mine is at the closed end. It does resemble a box canyon back home, doesn't it?"

"Can we maneuver down in there?" Elton asked. "In some places, it can't be more than a half-mile wide."

"We'll be pulling plenty of Gs," Johnson replied. "But think of the advantage we've got with all this steep-walled terrain around the target. It will confuse their radar returns. We'll be using the LANTIRN system and IR Mavericks, so we'll be able to see them, but they won't be able to see us. I think we're going to surprise the hell out of some Soviet scopeheads. We'll be in and out of there before they know what hit them."

"Isn't that what you said before the last mission?" Elton asked jokingly. "But we did pick up some iron, if I remember correctly. How did that happen?"

"That was then, this is now," Tom answered. "Let's do some serious flight planning. We've got a long night ahead of us."

After some intensive map study, they decided on a low level route for the flight. "We'll fly a heading of 069 degrees from Bitburg and cross the Rhine south of Koblenz," Dick said. "Then we bear right a bit to 074 degrees and fly to the edge of this little town, Hunfield. That will make

Drawings of AGM-65 Maverick show variants of seekers and warheads.

135

a good fix for our turn toward the railroad junction. The junction will show up real well on the radar, and we can leave it in freeze about then."

"Okay," Johnson agreed. "Then we whip a left turn to 045 degrees and head for the junction. Once there, we turn farther left to 330 degrees and hit the valley. Look—on the way to Hunfield, we'll have to skirt this town of Muhlhausen, and after Hunfeld, we'll fly pretty close to Haina, that airfield we hit. I wonder if the guy we shot down made it back to the field? He got a good chute when he punched out."

"If he did, he's probably waiting for us," Elton said. "But he'll never find us. The Foxbat has the wrong radar for low-level targets."

"True," Johnson replied, "but his Archer missiles are built for terminal self-guidance. If he should trigger one off in the right direction, it just might find us. We'll just keep a close watch on our six o'clock."

"Let's think about the flight," Elton said. "Generally, we fly northeast to the junction and then turn northwest to fly to the valley." He fed some figures

136   *High-flying Lockheed TR-1 reconnaissance aircraft collected electronic and other intelligence information about the TVD command train.*

into his hand-held navigation computer. "The ingress will take 26 minutes, flying at 500 knots. Once we get there, how do you plan to handle the attack?"

"We'll fly right into the mouth of the little valley at 100 feet," Tom said. "Once we see the train with the FLIR, I'll position us to attack. We don't know where their defenses are, so our tactics will have to be subject to modification, as the bureaucrats say. We'll play it by ear, depending on what we're up against. But we can tell on the map that the tracks hug the eastern wall of the valley. So I'll try to make the first attack by turning left off our entry heading 45 degrees or so. We'll designate the engine as the target for one Maverick, and we'll pick a spot halfway down the train for another. Then I'll fly as close to the left-hand canyon wall as we can get without scraping a wingtip, and turn hard right toward the train. We'll be too low and close for their SAMs to work."

Elton diagrammed the attack on a piece of paper. "Coming around in a right-hand turn, and assuming the train backed onto the spur and into the valley, we'll see the target halfway down the train in the FLIR field of view first," he pointed out. "Then, as we continue the turn, the engine will come into view. So we'll designate the midpoint for the first Maverick and the engine for the second."

"Right," Tom agreed. "After that, we'll stay in the valley, avoiding the ZSU-23s and 57mm stuff as well as we can, and dodge any SAMs they might send up. We'll see what our Mavericks blow up and go after what's left. I'll try to fire two Mavericks on each pass, giving us three passes. Then, if things haven't gotten too hot, we'll make one final pass, rear to front of the train, and rip 'em up with the gun."

137

"And after that, we'll haul ass, right?" asked Elton with a smile.

"You got it," agreed Johnson. "Hotel Alpha, as they say in the infantry. Now, let's work on the egress route. We'll come out low and fast, and be back for breakfast."

The two men bent over the planning table. The detailed flight and attack planning would take several hours. At 0245 hours, two hours before takeoff time, they received their final briefing from Falatchik.

Falatchik was eager to pass on the good words. "We have confirmation the train is definitely located in the valley," he said. "Classic SAM and ZSU dispositions around it. Good hunting."

Johnson, Elton and the backup crew suited up and were driven to their aircraft. Sergeant Jennifer Collins saluted and reported the aircraft ready to fly. On the ramp, Colonel Crawford also waited, wanting to talk to them before they started their walkaround inspection.

"This is probably the most important target you'll ever hit," he said. "We've knocked down all their airborne command and control aircraft. Knocking out their supreme commander will really destroy their operational command and control."

"We'll get in and burn them," said Johnson.

"Damn right. I know you will. Now, you know why we're sending a single," Crawford continued. "We're sending one aircraft because you'll have a better chance of getting in undetected. A big attacking force would only bring up all their air defenses. After you attack, you know the codeword to tell the AWACS birds the results. If you don't succeed, we'll have to send in a daylight attacking force to get that train. We'll get it, sure. But in the process, we'll lose some birds and some good jocks. So do your usual good job and get back safely. We're starting to consider you as family."

"No sweat," Johnson said reassuringly, and he shook hands with Crawford. He and Elton turned to the task of preflighting their weapons, secure in knowing that Jennifer Collins had the airplane ready to fly.

As the two airmen joined Sergeant Collins under the left wing, Colonel Crawford reflected on other missions; the countless times when he had sent young airmen aloft into peril, and in earlier years, when he himself had been dispatched into the darkness.

From long experience, he knew that fighter jocks who begin to worry about not making it back are no longer effective fighter pilots. The ones with the most self-confidence are the ones who make it. Johnson and Elton were the kind of jocks who come back.

139

Slipping In

Gorshkov Scrambles for Round Two

They thanked Crawford and turned to the task at hand. Johnson checked the Mavericks mounted under the wings on stations 2 and 8. A pylon extended down from each wing station. At the end of each pylon was a launcher on which were mounted three Mavericks. He removed the protective covers from the nose of each missile and made sure the IR dome was clear and uncracked. Inside each dome, he could see the gyro optics assembly, its intricate parts gleaming. He replaced each protective cover.

Then he checked the four AMRAAM air-to-air missiles mounted on either side of each pylon just above the Mavericks. He patted the AMRAAMs, remembering how well missiles like these had performed against yesterday's Soviet fighters. Completing his walkaround inspection, he climbed into the cockpit. Elton was already in his seat. As before, Sergeant Collins assisted Johnson as he strapped in. She wished them both luck and climbed down, saluting as the aircraft rolled.

At Haina, Colonel Gorshkov and his wingman strapped into their MiG-25s, parked and ready

in alert positions just off the end of the runway. They were part of the alert force intended to repel an attack, if one came, on the Western TVD Command Train. The Soviet High Command did not know if the NATO side had determined the location of the train, but had to prepare for the worst case. In their view, that would be a large, massed, NATO air attacking force striking at dawn.

So Gorshkov and other alerted crews were positioned now, their birds armed and ready. At other fields and in the air, Su-27 Flankers and MiG-29 Fulcrums waited. Gorshkov anticipated a long, cold two hours of sitting in a total blackout waiting for an attack that might not come until morning.

Supplied with electrical power through an umbilical cord from a diesel-engined flight line generator that his crew chief had wheeled into position beside his aircraft, he listened on the alert frequency for either order: launch or standdown. From time to time, like alert pilots in any air force, he briefly closed his eyes,

Between missions, ground crew members can open 185 access doors on the F-15. More than 85 percent can be reached without a stepladder.

While aircrews and ground staff prepared for the day's mission, high above Central Europe an E-3A Sentry AWACS aircraft refueled from a KC-135 tanker.

squirmed into different positions in his seat, adjusted his helmet and mask, drummed his fingers on the canopy rail, ran his hands over the cockpit switches, mentally reviewed his flight procedures -- anything to keep himself occupied. Because of the blackout, he could not pass the time reading. He was grateful for a small tarpaulin his crew chief had rigged over the canopy to keep the night dampness at bay. The usual central East Germany overcast hung a thousand feet above the field.

At 0430, Johnson and Elton taxied out to the Bitburg ALARS. As before, LANTIRN transformed the blackness outside into daylight in the HUD. As they taxied, Johnson checked out the Maverick and AMRAAM electronics while Elton initiated the built-in checks in the aircraft electronics and made sure the inertial navigation system velocities were within tolerances.

For this mission, they had activated the Strike Eagle's Tactical Situation Display, which each crewman elected to call up on his right-hand Multipurpose Color Display. The TSD presented a moving picture of a large-scale map exactly like the one they had used for flight planning. A small "stick figure" aircraft on the face of the display, called the Current Aircraft Position Indicator, showed their exact position in relation to geographical features on and near their flight path.

Either crew member could update the TSD in flight, if necessary, by designating visual checkpoints, by radar returns or navigation radio fixes. Checkpoints, alternate checkpoints, aimpoints and the target had been programmed into the system through the Data Transfer Module. Johnson had inserted the DTM into its slot in the front cockpit instrument panel after he had lowered himself into his seat. The map itself, on a roll of color film, had been inserted into its receptacle on the rear cockpit right console by Dick Elton.

143

As they flew, the map would scroll along, like a strip map, and the Current Aircraft Position Indicator would show their exact location. The map and the position indicator were commanded by the aircraft computer, using inputs from the INS. Now, as they taxied, the little aircraft overlay Bitburg Air Base. It changed orientation, but not position, on the map as Tom released brakes and turned the aircraft out of the parking space, across the ramp, and onto the taxiway.

They felt the cockpit bob up and down, like a Cadillac on a slightly bumpy road, as they taxied over the uneven taxiway leading out to the ALARS.

Su-27 Flanker fighter-interceptor was a match for the best NATO fighters in aerial combat. Its look-down, shoot-down capability was lacking in the MiG-25 Foxbat.

144

Even "dumb" iron bombs like these can be dropped more accurately from F-15E. Up to 24 Mk 82 500-pounders can be carried.

Tom turned onto the concrete runway, which had been "toned down" with painted earth colors to make it hard to see from the air. Aided by the FLIR, he lined up on the takeoff heading, ran the RPM to 80 percent and checked out the systems and engines.

"Ready to fly?" he asked Dick.

"Ready to fly," Dick responded. Tom released the brakes and the big Strike Eagle surged forward. The crew felt a thump as the wheels passed over the runway's approach end arresting cable.

The takeoff was exactly like the previous day's experience—up to a point. But this time, however, when Tom pushed the throttles up to the military power limits, he did not stop. He pushed them through the detents into afterburner range. The additional thrust immediately took effect. They felt the aircraft leap forward as if slung from a giant slingshot. The rapid acceleration firmly pushed them back in their seats.

Tom observed the afterburner nozzle indicator needles on the instrument panel move to the closed position as he advanced the throttles through full military power, and then saw them unwind to "open" as the system cycled through all five stages of afterburner. The air conditioning system hissed as it controlled the climate in the cockpit.

The night around the aircraft was suddenly lit up by the hot white light from the engines, jetting raw power from the flaming afterburners. Both flyers experienced the exhilaration of the tremendous acceleration. They quickly reached the acceleration check speed and then nosewheel lift-off speed.

Tom raised the nose. When the slight bumping of the landing gear over the uneven runway stopped abruptly, they knew they were airborne in the night. As Tom had advanced the throttles to the full afterburner position, he simply kept his hand moving, lifting it off the throttles, to reach forward to the instrument panel for the landing gear actuator handle. Almost immediately, he flipped it up, and then raised the flaps.

In the time required to take a couple of breaths, they were accelerating through 350 knots and

Front and rear cockpits of F-15E simulator. WSO has four displays active; center left is an infrared image; right center is a radar image of an airfield many miles ahead.

leveling at 500 feet above the terrain. Tom retarded the throttles out of afterburner range and rolled into a hard right turn around to their course heading. When the airspeed reached 500 knots, he reduced the power setting to hold it and prepared to descend to 100 feet above the terrain. The slipstream sang its roaring song, dimly audible to both flyers, sealed under the protection of the clear canopy. The Current Aircraft Position Indicator showed they were speeding past their sister base, Spangdahlem.

Tom eased the stick forward and the Strike Eagle descended rapidly to 100 feet above the rolling Eifel terrain. Looking through the HUD with the FLIR, Tom could see some of the scars from the previous evening's air battle. Here and there, smoking pieces of aircraft wreckage littered the hills and fields.

"Looks like a bird crashed into that castle," he commented to Elton.

Dick viewed the FLIR through one of his MCPDs. "Right," he commented. "Hope the civilians weren't hurt."

"Civilians," Tom responded, "the innocent casualties of war."

As planned, they flashed across the Rhine southeast of Koblenz. They entered the corridor leading into Soviet territory, speeding northeast of Fulda. They saw the devastation of battle on the ground everywhere, but took no friendly ground fire. Tom changed course several times to avoid both friendly and enemy helicopters droning cautiously through the darkness across his flight path. As soon as they were across the Forward Line of Troops, however, the quiet situation changed. Tracers, red and green, began to crisscross the sky and anti-aircraft bursts flamed like giant, sinister fireflies in the blackness. Soviet air defenders were opening up blindly, alerted by the roar of the Strike Eagle's powerful engines. Occasionally, a lucky near burst rocked the aircraft. To the right and left, other batteries opened up, their operators spooked by the sound and sight of those guns already firing. Most tracers curved behind their fleeting craft, then disappeared into the overcast.

147

"They can hear us, but they can't see us," Tom said, "not even on radar."

"Right," Dick responded. "They only know where we've been, but not where we're going. Just the same, that doesn't mean one of 'em won't fire the 'Golden Beebee' that zaps us."

"Our luck will hold," Johnson said tersely. Silently, he said a short prayer. *I ought to spend more time in church with the family,* he thought. He zigzagged right and left, generally following their planned course line, but never keeping the same heading for more than five or 10 seconds. "You can bet these people on the ground are reporting us to their air defense net." He dipped into a small stream valley, and tracers from hilltops crisscrossed above them. They flashed out of the valley and under some high tension transmission wires. Tom kept his attention on the HUD, eyes flicking occasionally to the instrument panel and map display. They roared by the small city of Muhlhausen, staying well clear of the town perimeter.

"Let's arm up," Johnson commanded. On the Master Mode switches under the HUD, Tom selected Air to Ground. Using a menu displayed on his left hand MPD, he pressed a button to activate the Mavericks. He selected stations 2 and 8, and the display read "Standby" for both stations.

"Okay," said Tom. "Remember our planning. I handle station 2 and you handle station 8. Two missiles each pass. I launch mine and then you launch yours."

"Right," said Elton. "Hit the Master Arm switch." Tom actuated the switch, and the missile status on the display soon changed from "Standby" to "Ready." They slipped by Hunfeld, and Johnson racked the bird into a hard left turn. He rolled out heading for the railroad junction, only 65 miles—and less than eight minutes—away.

148

At Haina, Colonel Gorshkov stiffened as his radio headset came alive. "Scramble! Fast mover approaching at low altitude from the southwest." Gorshkov and his wingman started their engines. The ground crews performed their duties and stepped back. In less than two minutes, the two MiG-25s were airborne in close formation. Jester One-One was passing a point directly in line with the Haina takeoff runway, 10 miles away. But Gorshkov's radar did not show a target, only ground clutter.

"Redstar Two-One airborne," he radioed. "Request vectors."

His ground controller quickly responded. "We do not have a radar target. Reports on the bogey are being relayed into the air defense center by telephone from ground observers. Turn to a heading of 360 and climb to 1,000 meters. Do not exceed 1,000 meters. You have other interceptors above you." The Soviet leader followed instructions, accelerating as he climbed. The two aircraft, external lights blacked out, entered the thin overcast and soon popped out on top. As

149

While Gorshkov in his MiG-25 awaited the signal to scramble, MiG-23s like this also sat on alert status at tactical airstrips.

they started their climb, Gorshkov's wingman fell back into a staggered trail position and maintained it by painting his leader on radar. Redstar flight's radar emissions gave away their position to anyone with the right equipment.

In the backseat of the Strike Eagle, with all emitters on Standby, Elton monitored the Tactical Electronic Warning System indicators. "I've got two airborne emitters ten miles off our right wing. By the type of radar signal they're putting out, I'd say they're Foxbats."

"Shit Hot!" said Johnson. "They don't have a low-level fighting capability. They won't see us."

"No," said Elton. "But they're probably the first flight to be scrambled after us. There are bound to be others. The Soviets know that train is a juicy target."

"Yeah," Tom answered, "but they don't know yet that we're after it. They probably expect a big strike. They won't commit numbers until they're sure we're after the train. We'll be there before they can react." He rolled into a sharp right bank as another line of tracers futilely reached out for them and some 57mm bursts exploded just behind them, momentarily lighting up the cockpit. Both men involuntarily flinched. The adrenalin was really flowing now, and they were breathing faster.

"Redstar Two-One," the controller radioed to Gorshkov after a minute. "Still no radar contact. The bogey is reported moving northeast beneath your position. Do you have a visual contact?"

Gorshkov looked down. He saw nothing but blackness and the lights of towns barely shining through the undercast—and then he saw bursts of tracers and anti-aircraft fire.

"That must be directed at the bogey," he reasoned. He could not see his target, but he could see where it had been. He turned northeast. Almost immediately, he saw groundfire off his left wing. "That's him," Gorshkov told himself, and turned left.

Johnson had jinked left after the last burst. He now turned right, across his planned ingress route. On the deck, he passed undetected under Gorshkov, who was thousands of feet above him. Other batteries, spooked, were now opening up, showing Gorshkov a broad pattern that indicated no particular flight direction for the intruder.

The TSD showed Jester One-One was approaching the railroad junction. In the HUD, Johnson could already see a small lake just south of the intersection. "Armament check," he called on intercom.

Elton called, "Master Arm on. Armament and Air to Ground selected. AGM-65 selected on stations 2 and 8. Weapons one and two selected, and they are armed."

151

Above them in the blackness, Gorshkov zigzagged back and forth, following vectors from his ground controller that were always too late. He then decided to fly to a position over the command train and enter an orbit at his assigned altitude, 1,000 meters, or about 3,300 feet. His inertial navigation system indicated the general area of the train. Perhaps he could cover it from here.

Down in the Valley

Command Train Attacked

Above Gorshkov, Su-27 Flankers were vectored into the area. Elton checked the TEWS display and saw the symbology. "We have both MiG-25s and Su-27s above us," he reported to Tom.

"And above us is where they better stay," Johnson grunted in reply.

The leader of the first flight of Su-27s, even with look-down, shoot-down radar, was frustrated. His controller reported a low bogey. He could not see the bogey on his display, but he could see Gorshkov's flight, which had been identified for him by the controller. He was picking up lots of clutter. The MiG-25s were only at 1,000 meters, he knew. How low could this assumed NATO aircraft be—especially in the pitch black darkness?

The Strike Eagle roared over the railroad junction. Johnson rolled hard left and felt his G-suit inflate and grip his torso and legs. He rolled out on a heading of 330 degrees. They were flying right up the spur line toward the narrow valley entrance. He pushed up the throttles and felt the bird accelerate to 540 knots. The slipstream roared

louder, barely audible to the airmen in the cockpit.

On the train in the valley, Kalishni and his crew were alerted by the air defense network to the approach of the bogey, which was now assumed to be an attacker. All sensors were up and pointed skyward.

"Do you have a contact yet?" he telephoned to the SAM senior controller on the high ground above the valley.

"No contact," the controller reported. "Could we have a false alarm?"

"Possible but not likely," Kalishni replied. "Too many ground observer reports. Something is approaching, and it is coming fast."

At that moment, the Strike Eagle blasted through the valley entrance. Johnson racked the bird into a vertical right bank and then snapped the wings back level with the nose pointed north up the tracks toward the train. With the FLIR, he could see a valley that might have been in the Swiss Alps. To his right, the swift little stream that over the centuries had carved the valley coursed along the east wall. As depicted on the planning chart,

Imaging infrared Maverick missile enables F-15E crew to blast armored targets at night. Infrared seeker creates an image of the scene based on heat emissions. Weapon systems operator or pilot in F-15E use infrared image to guide Maverick to the target.

153

the railroad spur edged the banks of the stream. Small chalets and farm houses dotted the verdant valley floor. Smaller buildings, like miniature barns, were filled with fodder for livestock. Here and there to his left, small brooks rushed down the steep west wall and coursed along the valley floor to join the main stream.

Tom flicked a glance at the engine instruments. Both were rotating at full military power: 93 percent. Hunched forward in their seats, Johnson and Elton covered the six miles to the train in less than 45 seconds. They were abeam the train and into the attack turn before the roar of their engines alerted Kalishni and his crews to their presence. Several of the Soviets' radars picked up the Strike Eagle briefly, but because it was so low, they had it within their lethal horizons and on their scopes only momentarily. They began to fire blindly into the overcast, and Kalishni's eardrums were battered by the din. The only result of their muzzle blasts was a thin pall of smoke which began to drift through the valley.

Johnson rolled left toward the west valley wall as soon as he saw the train through the HUD. He could see the emplacements were pretty widely dispersed. At the same time, with a glance, he identified the target on the Maverick display. Elton had it on his display in the rear cockpit as well.

"I'm going to designate the middle car on the train," Tom said. Using his finger to move the Target Designator Control on the inboard throttle, he slewed the targeting symbols over one of Kalishni's two generator cars and depressed the button to designate the target for the first Maverick.

As the Strike Eagle angled toward the valley wall, he began a sweeping, slightly climbing right turn to bring the nose—and the Maverick's seeker eye—around toward the train. As the distance

to the target decreased, the triangular range caret moved down the face of the display. The Strike Eagle was well within firing range and the Shoot Cue began to flash as the target came into the field of view. Tom stopped the climb at 500 feet. This enabled some of the Soviet radars to paint their aircraft for several seconds, so Elton actuated the jamming equipment. It worked. The furious fire was aimed behind them.

Johnson entered a shallow dive and thumbed the weapon release button on top of the stick.

"Now!" he grunted. The Maverick leaped off the launcher under the left wing and flashed toward the target. The Strike Eagle was momentarily bathed in the glare of the missile's rocket engine as it whooshed away. The slight odor of burning rocket fuel permeated the cockpit briefly. "Your turn!" Johnson said to Elton.

Dick Elton followed the same procedure as Johnson, slewed the symbology over the train's engine, locked on, and launched his missile. They were already turning right, away from the train, toward the valley wall, when Johnson's

Sequence of Maverick   155
missile in operation.

Maverick's solid rocket motor zips the fat missile at supersonic speed.

missile impacted the generator car. The eight-foot Maverick penetrated the side of the car and then the shaped charge exploded, tearing the guts out of the diesel engine powering the generating equipment.

A bright red flash edged with yellow erupted as the car was blasted over on its side. It began to burn fiercely.

Kalishni, who had been leaning out of the open window of his car, trying to divine the position of the attacker, involuntarily withdrew at the sound of the explosion, which was followed by a rolling blast of heat.

A moment later, Elton's Maverick slammed into the engine, drilling low into its huge internal fuel tanks. They exploded with a roar, and their fierce orange glow lit up the valley's east wall like a sunrise. The convulsing explosions that followed rocked the entire train. Dirty black smoke, the signature of a diesel fuel fire, was vomited upward mixing into the overcast. Kalishni was thrown to the floor of his car, but leaped up and ran into his command module. "Get them! Get them!"

he shouted into the phone to his SAM controller.

"Comrade General," the controller replied from his high vantage point, "we cannot paint the target from up here. We are looking down into too much ground return. You must depend on the anti-aircraft batteries on the valley floor."

Kalishni ground his teeth as he realized how badly he had planned the disposition of his SAMs. They were positioned for an attack from above, not at Strike Eagle altitude, well below the level of the sites. On the other hand, he did not know that, even if the most capable SAMs were positioned on the valley floor, it would be all but impossible for them to lock onto an F-15 streaking along at near supersonic speed on the treetops.

"Right on target!" Johnson said.

Outside Kalishni's car, the anti-aircraft guns were firing wildly, filling the sky with hot splintered steel, but the Strike Eagle was beyond their lethal horizons as Johnson and Elton prepared for their second run.

"Select three and four," Johnson ordered through tight lips.

Targets as distant as 15 miles can be engaged by Maverick, and blasted with its 300-pound warhead.

157

"They're ready to go," Elton reported.

Tom flew close to the west wall, preparing to start his right turn, and now designated the second command module car as the next Maverick target. Elton picked out a car farther back on the train, which happened to be the munitions supply car. On the train, the fire from the engine had spread back through the anti-aircraft car, setting off towering explosions fed by the ammunition on board. Kalishni knew his personal car was about to be burned to a cinder. He ran back into the command module car.

Above them, cursing, Gorshkov flew his frustrated orbit. His controller had told him an attack by an unknown number of bandits was underway.

He could see the glow of the burning train piercing the cloud layer beneath him. He knew the overcast probably did not extend all the way to the ground. Gorshkov decided to get down under it and hope for light from the burning train to show him the attacker -- and the terrain. He knew the valley ran north-south. The glowing fire and explosions gave him his exact location. He retarded his throttles, lowered the nose, and making sure he was on an exact south heading, began his descent.

"I am descending into the valley," he radioed to his controller. "Inform the defending forces so that their SAMs don't kill me by mistake."

"Keep orbiting," he told his wingman. "It is too dangerous for both of us to be so low in those

Su-27 pilots had to remain above the scene as Johnson and Elton roared into the valley at 100 feet.

confined quarters."

Higher up, the pilot of the lead Su-27 had briefly seen the Strike Eagle as a blip on his radar display when Johnson popped up to 500 feet above the valley floor. But then he lost him as Johnson descended. Now he watched Gorshkov's blip on his display as he descended into the valley and

MiG-25E version of the Foxbat was especially deadly when it was armed with the AA-10 missile. The aircraft was not especially maneuverable in a dogfight, but the missile was unerring in seeking its target.

161

the ground clutter. Both blips had looked exactly the same on his digital display.

As Gorshkov entered the clouds, Johnson and Elton began their second run. As they started the turn around toward the target, Dick, monitoring the TEWS display, said, "We've got a MiG-25 in close." He could not tell Gorshkov's altitude because the Strike Eagle radar was in standby mode.

"He'll never get down in this valley without killing himself," Tom replied. "He's not equipped for it."

"He must know that. Maybe he's got more balls than brains," Elton tersely answered.

"They must be brass," said Tom. Unknowingly, he had just described the Soviet wing commander to a tee. In Gorshkov's years of fighter flying, audacity and luck, more than anything else, had kept him alive.

Tom released his second Maverick. Dick's followed two seconds later. Tom's Maverick slammed into the second command module car as its exploding warhead drove shaped hot metal fragments into the electronics equipment and the bodies of the operators. Equipment parts ricocheted around the room. Gaping holes were torn in the walls and ceiling. The force of the explosion lifted the car up in the air and broke it in half. The incinerating pieces tumbled to earth like a giant's broken toys.

A hot white fire broke out and scorched the other command car. Bodies and pieces of bodies were hurled in all directions. Inside the other command module car, which was shaking from the explosions, Kalishni could smell burning insulation and charred flesh. Equipment operators began to stampede toward the doorway at either end of the car.

"Stay at your posts!" he commanded. Nobody obeyed. "You are deserting in the face of the enemy!" They kept moving out the doorways. He was soon alone. The first flicker of fear began to course through his body, but he decided to remain at his post.

Elton's Maverick plowed dead center into the munitions stores for the entire train and triggered a giant, erupting explosion that flattened the cars on either side and blistered the earth for a quarter mile around. "Bingo!" Dick said. "Two more hits! It's 4th of July in Germany." The fires of the crippled train lit up the low overcast.

Johnson and Elton banked away, still two safe miles from the target. At that moment, Gorshkov, brass balls and all, descended out of the clouds at their three o'clock high position. They momentarily entered a jinking right bank. For an instant, outlined against the burning train, the Soviet fighter pilot saw the unmistakable long, graceful, daggerlike nose, squared off engine intakes and sharply swept wings and notched tailplanes of the Strike Eagle.

"An F-15!" he said aloud to himself. "And in these circumstances, at such a low altitude, it can only be an F-15. Perhaps from the same squadron as the one that shot me down yesterday." The thought made him angry. He checked his armament switches and made sure his missiles were armed. But before he could react further, his aircraft was rocked by bracketing anti-aircraft bursts from Kalishni's air defense crews. He quickly broke away to escape being shot down.

"Idiots!" he shouted. "I'm on your side!" Nevertheless, now demoralized and frightened air defenders were reacting to their first target. Gorshkov, at 400 feet above the valley floor, was easily detectable on the fire control radars. The crews did not know how many attackers they were up against. All they knew was that the high-value target they were supposed to protect was systematically being blown to pieces. Gorshkov realized he had been lucky that the SAM sites had not fired on him as he descended.

In the valley, the high ground around him prevented Gorshkov from communicating with his controller, so he radioed his wingman to pass on the information that at least one of the attackers—maybe the only attacker—was a Strike Eagle. The leader of the Su-27 flight also heard the transmission.

Meanwhile, the F-15 disappeared into the blackness, streaking down the tracks in the direction of the valley entrance. Before reaching it, Johnson pulled hard into a right turn back toward the train, then let the momentum carry the aircraft out toward the west valley wall. This time, they would hit the train from front to rear, attacking in the direction opposite the first two attacks. It was not exactly what they had planned, but circumstances now dictated they be flexible.

Gorshkov could not see the wall, but he could almost feel it. He slewed his radar, looking for a contact. He tried boresighting it and turned in the direction he thought the Strike Eagle must be. But it was too low. Nothing but ground return. Auto-acquisition did not work either.

Now 500 feet above the ground and just beneath the overcast, Gorshkov turned left toward the tracks to give himself plenty of clearance from the unseen west wall, and then started a right turn which brought him inside the path followed by Johnson and Elton as they flew a reciprocal course, parallel to their last attack heading. Now they saw him! He was outlined against the overcast, which reflected the distant glow from the burning train! His silhouette was unmistakable.

"MiG-25 at three o'clock, slightly high!" Elton said. The pitch of his voice had gone up a bit.

"Sonofabitch!" Johnson said. "Doesn't he know he can't operate down here? I don't think he can see us. Anything on the TEWS?"

"He's still in search mode," Elton replied. "He can't see us in this blackness. Looks like he's trying to find us but can't. Probably picking up nothing but ground clutter."

"Look! Flak!" cried Johnson. "His own people are peppering him! They must be really shook up!" They saw Gorshkov bank away and be quickly swallowed up by the darkness.

They started the pop up and final turn in. Above, the Su-27 leader's radar was intermittently painting two targets. Which, he wondered, was the attacker, and which was Gorshkov?

As the F-15 climbed to missile release altitude, both Americans were breathing hard. Four eyes were on the target displays, and educated fingers were designating impact points for the last two Mavericks. For the moment, the two airmen concentrated on the train. The MiG-25 would have to wait.

Elton flicked glances toward the TEWS display. Johnson picked out the second command module car and Elton designated the second supply car for his Maverick. They began their dive, released their missiles, and banked away, still safe in the darkness and out of range of defending ground fire.

In the command module car, Kalishni stood alone, staring wildly at empty chairs and blank displays. The overhead lights flickered. Then there was a thunderous crash as Johnson's third Maverick sliced into the car and exploded. General Kalishni, brightest star in the Soviet strategic firmament, was decapitated, incinerated and blown away in an instant. Seconds later, Elton's bird impacted near the rear of the train, igniting another SAM cache which exploded like an erupting volcano.

The Soviet Western TVD Command Train was out of action. Permanently.

Fighting Their Way Out

Flankers and Foxbats on the Attack

"Scratch one train!" Johnson said briskly. Then he depressed the mike button on the inboard side of the throttle with his left thumb and called in the blind: "Smashup, smashup, smashup! I say again, smashup, smashup, smashup."

There was no answer, but the message was received on-board the listening NATO AWACS aircraft in its orbit high above West Germany. Maj. Gen. Lou Donnelly, the airborne commander on-board the big Sentinel, had been hunched intently over the UHF radio console for the last half hour, waiting for Johnson to check in. He smiled broadly when he heard the words. He immediately retransmitted a coded message to Headquarters, U.S. Air Forces Europe, at Ramstein, and to Bitburg: "The Soviet Western TVD Command Train was destroyed."

There was elation all down the command chain, and scores of strike fighters that had been waiting for the launch order to attack the train were now ordered to attack their secondary targets.

Colonel Crawford, in the dimly lit command post at Bitburg, felt a surge of elation, but it was quickly replaced with a feeling of concern as he thought of the job Johnson and Elton still faced —fighting their way out. He took consolation in one thought—no other deep penetration strike aircraft could perform the mission like the Strike Eagle and be as survivable, so Johnson and Elton had the best chance possible of coming back.

But in the Strike Eagle cockpit, there was no time for elation. It was, instead, air battle time. Tension was higher than ever. Elton could feel his pulse pounding as he consciously slowed his breathing to prevent the onset of hyperventilation. Johnson punched the air-to-air Master Mode button at the top of the instrument panel. He watched the planform of his aircraft, showing the position of the four AMRAAMs, appear on the armament display on the left-hand MPD. The AMRAAM symbology appeared in the HUD. The air-to-air birds had been warming up in Standby since he had actuated the Master Arm switch at the start of the attack. Now the AMRAAM display showed missiles one and two, on the left and right pylons, armed and ready. He racked the Strike Eagle around in a gut-wrenching turn to a southerly heading. Now the west wall was off their right wing.

"Get me a target," he ordered crisply.

"Our emissions will show them where we are," Elton reminded him.

"Yeah, but we'll kill them before they can kill us," Johnson said. "Power up!" On the ridges, the Soviet SAM operators searched in vain on their scopes for their target, still down in the valley.

Elton switched the Hughes APG-70 high resolution radar out of Standby and put it on six-bar scan. On the first sweep of the antenna, the display showed Gorshkov on the left, almost off the scope, just above their altitude. Although the

167

Soviet pilot did not know it, he was turning into them in the darkness, only a mile away. Then the Strike Eagle's antenna swept again, tilted upward this time, and Elton picked up Gorshkov's wingman and, on the next sweep, the two Flankers above him.

"One bogey, probably the Foxbat, going from our two to three o'clock, slightly high," he reported.

Johnson divided his gaze between the HUD, with its daylight view of the outside world, and the front cockpit radar display.

"Another bogey at 3,300 feet, twelve o'clock high," Elton continued, "and two other bogeys, Flankers, at 10,000 feet, also twelve o'clock high. The bogey on the left is heading dead on, only about a mile away. The other three are heading north, also dead on. Nobody's locked on or launched anything yet, but I'm beginning to feel a little boxed in."

As he spoke, all four bandits passed through the bottom of the radar display as they moved toward the Strike Eagle's six o'clock position.

"No sweat," Johnson said. "The three above probably can't see us down where we are in the clutter, and Brass Balls, here, is too close to fire an Archer. Let's try to get a bead on a couple of the birds heading north." He held the southerly heading for another 15 seconds to open the range between him and the Soviet fighters. Then he rolled hard left and climbed to 500 feet above the valley floor. As he brought the nose around through a heading of east-northeast, he picked up the Flankers again on the edge of the display.

"I'm going for Flanker number two," he told Elton, "and then the low target, the Foxbat." Quickly, he positioned the acquisition symbols over the target Flanker and depressed the TDC button. The AMRAAM symbology showed they were at the Flanker wingman's five o'clock, well

within maximum range. The shoot cues in the display and on the canopy bow flashed. They had practically no overtake speed. The target was on the left-hand side of the display, but well within the AMRAAM's field of view. Tom firmly thumbed the weapon release button on the control stick. "Now!"

The AMRAAM was ejected from its launcher under the left wing, the rocket motor fired with a roar, and the missile shot straight ahead, then angled sharply upward and to the left, punching into the overcast. Momentarily, the intense white flame from its rocket engine illuminated the Strike Eagle and then became a white glow in the clouds as the missile penetrated the overcast.

"Fox One!" called Tom. Not waiting for missile impact, Tom positioned the acquisition symbols over the blip that was Gorshkov's wingman and launched the second AMRAAM. It whooshed away from its position under the right wing and climbed swiftly into the overcast.

Guided unerringly by the Strike Eagle's radar and then by its own terminal guidance system,

NATO AWACS airplane, the E-3A Sentry, was a vital link in control of the battles on the Central Front.

169

the first AMRAAM rose like an avenger from the darkness below, adjusted its flight attack course slightly, and struck the Flanker on the right side, just aft of the wing. The pilot saw the flame of its rocket motor out of the corner of his eye, but he did not have time to react before his aircraft was blasted by the AMRAAM. In an instant, he was engulfed in flames as his fuel tanks ignited. The right wing was blown from its shoulder mount on the fuselage, and the engines began to disintegrate. He did not even have time for a radio call before he ejected into the icy blackness.

The lead Flanker pilot saw the explosion. "My wingman has been shot down!" he radioed to his controller. "I can't tell if it was one of our own SAMs or an air-to-air weapon from the bogey. I am taking evasive action!" He actuated his on-board protection system and turned hard right in an evasive maneuver. But Johnson wasn't after him.

Gorshkov's young wingman watched in fascinated horror as he saw the first AMRAAM streak out of the undercast and home in on one of the orbiting Flankers, ahead and thousands of feet above him. He watched the missile's impact on the Flanker wingman's aircraft and the resulting flames and explosion. With some relief, he saw the brief trail of the ejection seat rocket as it angled away from the doomed Flanker, telling him that the pilot had gotten out.

He was still gazing upward, openmouthed, when the second AMRAAM, which he never saw, slammed into the belly of his own craft. His first indication of impending doom was the ripping sound of impact and the vicious upward lunge of his aircraft, propelled by the detonating shaped warhead of the AMRAAM.

The missile punched a hole in the belly exactly midway between the two engines. The exploding warhead stripped the turbine sections out of them and blew away the afterburners and tailplanes. A sheet of flame from ruptured fuel tanks trailed behind the Foxbat hulk as it began to tumble in a downward arc toward the overcast. High negative Gs brutally forced the young pilot's head, arms and hands against the top of the canopy. Only leg restraints kept his lower limbs in place. He could not reach down into the cockpit to actuate the ejection system. For the first—and the last—time in his life, he felt the knife edge of terror in his gut as his aircraft tumbled over and over, enveloped in its own fireball, all the way down to its impact point in the forested mountains far below. A fountain of flame shot up from the crater, followed by a barrage of low order explosions as the Foxbat's ordnance cooked off. Then there was blackness.

Gorshkov, who had passed within a mile of the Strike Eagle without seeing it in the dark, looked over his shoulder when his peripheral vision caught the flaming missiles in their flight. Now he knew where the Strike Eagle was! Quickly, he carefully adjusted the tilt of his radar antenna to make it nearly level and began to execute a manual intercept. Grimly, grunting against the G forces, he racked his Foxbat into a hard turn around to bring it within missile firing parameters.

The two American airmen saw the flaming Soviet fighters plunge through the overcast and crash. Elton, monitoring the radar display, saw the remaining Flanker completing a 180-degree turn at 10,000 feet, putting him in position to bring his weapons to bear on the Strike Eagle. At the same time, he saw Gorshkov, near their altitude, starting his turn.

"We've got two with weapons bearing on us. Which one are you going to take first?" he asked.

"I don't think the Foxbat can paint us down

171

View through the HUD in an air-to-air fight. Enemy fighter is about to be dead. Engagement is at 15,900 feet, in a level plane and hard left turn.

172

here," Johnson replied. "Let's go for the high target first."

The lead Flanker was now painting two targets again. Which was the intruder? He watched as Gorshkov started a turn to the south and Johnson held his northerly course, but he could not distinguish which was his target. Two fighters are down, he thought. Don't just sit here —attack! He quickly designated one of the targets for his Archers and prepared to launch.

In the valley, Johnson, as before, designated the Flanker and launched his third AMRAAM, which climbed rapidly toward the target. A split second later, the Flanker pilot launched his first Archer. It plunged unerringly downward toward its target.

"He's launched a missile!" Elton hit the chaff dispenser and actuated the jamming system.

Gorshkov, close in, but still not too close to fire one of his own missiles, was suddenly able to see the Strike Eagle on his radar. "Now I have him!" he said aloud. He designated the target for his first Archer. The symbology changed and he got a Shoot indication. He was just pressing the firing button when the Flanker's Archer plunged into the top of his right wing and exploded. The Flanker pilot had chosen the wrong target. The Foxbat swerved violently to the left and began to roll.

Reacting immediately, Gorshkov, for the second time in two days, ejected. This time, he was only a few hundred feet above the valley floor and in a vertical bank. The trajectory of the ejection was parallel to the ground. His parachute, which began to deploy from behind the seat's headrest as Gorshkov was propelled out of the cockpit, blossomed only an instant before Gorshkov landed in a farmyard.

Miraculously, he was unhurt. His first emotion was relief at being alive. His second was a mixture of puzzlement and anger at having been shot down by . . . what? His own people? His third emotion was fury and disgust as he realized he had landed in a manure pile!

He could hear the engines of the Strike Eagle as it roared along the west wall of the valley, just above the treetops. In an instant, the sound had faded. He shook his fist at the sky. He would have vengeance on this Strike Eagle before this war ended. Then he unfastened his parachute harness and slithered out of the manure pile.

"Shit!" cried Gorshkov. "Shit, shit, SHIT!"

High above, the Flanker pilot saw Johnson's missile climbing toward him at terrific speed. He released a cloud of chaff, but the AMRAAM had already identified its target and was boring in. The Flanker pilot instinctively hauled back on the stick and began to zoom. The AMRAAM caught his aircraft squarely in the belly. The fuel tanks exploded and the aircraft disintegrated. There were no more targets on the Strike Eagle's radar display.

174

Another AMRAAM missile leaves an F-15, this time from a test aircraft of USAF's Armament Division at Eglin AFB, Florida.

"Let's go home," Johnson said. He racked the bird around into a turn to the south and, still at 100 feet, aimed for the valley opening.

On the heights, the acquisition radar for the Soviet SAM sites rotated endlessly. Operators were glued to their scopes, searching for a target they knew was there but could not be seen. The frustrated crews had seen only Soviet blips and they were now destroyed. The senior controller wondered how he would explain their inability to protect the most important point in the Soviet Western TVD.

Blasting out of the valley entrance, Johnson turned hard right and took up an easterly course. He reduced airspeed to 480 knots to conserve

fuel. "Battle damage?" he asked.

Elton scanned the instruments for system failures or signs of fluid leakages. None. "We got off without a scratch!" he reported.

"Right," said Johnson. "They can't hit what they can't see!"

At Soviet Air Defense Headquarters, word had been received of the Soviet Western TVD Command Train's destruction. The scores of fighters alerted to defend it were scrambled and vectored out to avenge the loss.

But they were vectored southwest, along the general track Johnson and Elton had followed on their ingress. But the Strike Eagle was exiting straight west, aiming at a point inside West

Germany just north of Kassel. Passing Nordhausen, the town on the main east-west railroad just west of the target area, they ran into the first tracers, ZSU-23 and larger anti-aircraft fire. As before, the Strike Eagle was past the danger zones by the time the defenders had begun firing.

Giving himself a chance to relax, Johnson put the aircraft on automatic terrain following, letting the systems fly it. Keeping a light hand on the stick, he monitored their progress as the aircraft climbed and descended, following the contours of the terrain below. The daylight world of the HUD revealed the devastation of the war. Bomb, missile and artillery craters dotted the landscape. Burned-out tank and armored personnel carriers were everywhere. Fires smoldered right and left of course. Bridges were collapsed into streams, and most of the roads were cut, especially at intersections. Railroad yards had been hit, and rolling stock had been destroyed as it stood on sidings. In contrast to the scene on the previous night's mission, all towns and villages were blacked out. Nobody wanted to be a target.

"It looks like they started something they wish they hadn't," Johnson said.

Elton had been watching the HUD scene on one of his displays in the back seat. "And I'll bet it will be a long time before they start something like this again."

"Could be, but don't forget—it's not over until it's over, and this is still just the beginning," Johnson added.

They flashed over the Leine River, just south of Gottingen, and they were back in friendly territory. They checked in with the AWACS and were directed to return to their home base, which was still intact. Johnson turned to the left, skirted Kassel, and took up a course for Bitburg. The adrenalin was still flowing, and they kept a sharp

177

scan for enemy aircraft.

By the time they reached Bitburg, the main runway had been repaired. They landed and taxied back in to their parking spot, where they were met by an ebullient Colonel Crawford. Jennifer Collins was delighted at the news of the three kills. In fact she had anticipated the

Information from the AWACS aircraft was transmitted to this German air defense center, then fused with other information to enable rational air defense decisions.

news and had a can of spray paint and a star template at the parking spot as they taxied in.

"Hey, we can't bring back three or four every day," Tom said.

They climbed down the ladder, and Johnson turned to shake Elton's hand. "A good night's work, right?" Elton smiled. "Jester work."

Colonel Crawford drove them back for the debriefings and the tired crew visited the Officer's Club, now open all night, for a hearty breakfast, and then retired to the BOQ to sleep. They knew there would be another target tonight.

178

Deep Strike Assigned

Jesters Teamed Up for Action

When they entered the briefing room that evening, Johnson and Elton paused as they saw their new strike mission laid out on the wall map. Elton gave a low whistle. The TPC E-2C Tactical Pilotage Chart, with a scale of 1:500,000, stretched from floor to ceiling. The course line started at Bitburg, in the lower left corner of the map. It angled all the way up across East Germany to the upper right hand corner, near Poland, where it ended on the Baltic Sea. Moving up close to the map, Elton read aloud the name of the termination point: "Peenemunde."

"Peenemunde. Isn't that the old Nazi missile center where they developed the V-2 ballistic missiles they launched at London during the closing days of World War II?" Johnson asked. "What's going on there now?"

"It has always been a test base," said Falatchik. "There's a big runway and extensive instrumented test ranges. In recent years at Peenemunde, they have tested just about every SAM and short range missile system the Soviets have developed."

"So we're going all that way to take out a new

SAM system," Johnson guessed.

"No. It's an aircraft," Falatchik said. "For the past two weeks, one of their big Antonov An-225 super heavylift transports has been based at Peenemunde, undergoing final testing."

"The Soviets call the An-225 the Myira," said Johnson. "I saw one of them at the Paris Air Show a couple of years ago. It flew into Le Bourget with that Soviet space shuttle, Buran, on top of it. The thing was really huge, a true manmade overcast. What's it carrying this time?"

"This is a one-of-a-kind bird with a giant microwave energy projector on board," answered Falatchik. "Only an aircraft this big could carry the kind of power-generating equipment needed to perform its mission."

"Which is?" Johnson asked.

"To flood the entire battle area with very high power microwave energy. It will jam, confuse or actually burn out all NATO electronic systems," Falatchik answered. "It can affect all kinds of electronics. With it, the Soviets could keep our control towers off the air, stopping operations at our airfields."

Johnson interrupted. "They could paralyze command and control centers, SAM sites, even tank columns. Aircraft radios and avionics could be knocked out, too. The Sentry AWACS would be zapped. Why, if this thing gets into action and is successful, we'll be flying blind, with no airborne command and control at all. And our birds, relying on all those integral electronics and avionics, could be crippled."

"Right," agreed Colonel Crawford. "Essentially, since we knocked down all their Candids yesterday morning, we have really screwed up their massed air offensive and defensive capability. We don't want that to happen to us."

Elton had been scrutinizing the map. He whistled

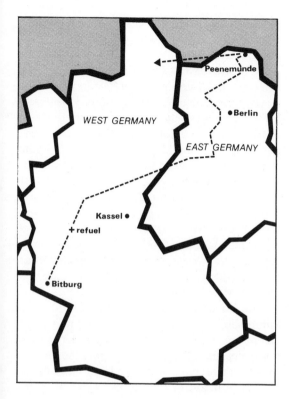

Aerial refueling extended Strike Eagle's legs for the long route to Peenemunde on the Baltic coast. Peenemunde was the site of Nazi rocket and missile research in the 1930s and 1940s. Its extensive facilities and remote location ensured that Peenemunde remained a prime R&D site after WW II and into the 1990s.

181

again. "It must be 400 miles from here to Peenemunde."

"Four hundred and thirty, to be exact," Colonel Crawford said. "It's a long haul on the deck, but the people at USAFE know the Strike Eagle can do it. You will take off and perform an inflight refueling right away to replace the gas you burned at high RPM on takeoff. Then you go down to a hundred feet above the terrain for the ingress."

Falatchik pointed to the ingress point. "They want you to enter enemy territory well south of a more direct, shorter route to Peenemunde so you don't tip off your destination. No other aircraft could carry out this low-level mission alone. The alternative is a massed raid with a lot of tanker support, or a strategic bomber commitment. The chance of losses is high for those options. What do you say?"

"We'll take the mission," Johnson replied. "If it can be done, Jesters can do it." He looked at the map closely. The color coding showed the terrain for the last part of the mission was low and flat.

"There's an awful lot of flat, low terrain during the last part of the flight," he said. "Even flying at 100 feet, we may be subjected to SAM attacks. Our on-board systems can probably handle them, but I'd feel better with some kind of suppression support."

"Glad you asked. I was coming to that," Colonel Crawford answered. "Your Jester squadron mates are going to provide suppression. The other three Strike Eagles at this base will be supporting you with AGM-136s."

"The Tacit Rainbow?" Johnson asked. "I'm impressed." The AGM-136, he knew, was death on emitters. He recalled the briefing at Bentwaters. It was designed to be launched from the ground or from an aircraft and fly to a loiter point in the air. There it would orbit until an enemy radar within its range began to emit signals. Immediately, the little missile would home in, dive and detonate its WDU-0 high-explosive, spherical shaped charge warhead into the site, using the emitting antenna as the aimpoint. The missile's IR signal and radar cross section were very small. It emitted no signals. It flew almost soundlessly. It was undetectable by known Soviet systems. A good little buddy to have on this mission.

"What's the employment concept?" Johnson asked.

"We'll have the other birds take off just ahead of you tonight," Colonel Crawford told them. "Each will fly along the border to an entry point into Pact territory. The northernmost point will be near Hamburg. The Jesters will ingress on the deck and fly to points west of your course. They will pop up and deploy their Tacit Rainbows. They will then descend back to the deck and withdraw back here. The AGM-136s will then fly on their own to preset loiter points. When a Pact radar comes up, an orbiting TR bird will detect it, home in on it, and kill it."

"How many of these Tango Romeo radar killers will be out there to protect us?" Elton asked.

"Each F-15 can carry nine of them," Crawford answered, "so you will have 27 AGM-136s to support you. We'll concentrate the force over the northernmost part of your route."

"Sounds good," Johnson and Elton chorused.

They sat down for Falatchik's briefing. Johnson looked around the room at the other airmen and smiled. It felt good to be briefing with the other Jesters that had flown into Bitburg on his wing. It was good to know they were all still alive. He was proud of these Jesters and the job they had been doing flying their lonely and tough missions. Every crew had shot down more than five Soviet

Il-76 Candid, modified with a dorsal radome, served as a mini-AWACS for Warsaw Pact forces. Although larger in volume, its electronic capabilities were about the same as the US Navy's E-2C Hawkeye aircraft.

183

Tacit Rainbow unmanned aircraft (AGM-136) was developed by the US Air Force to loiter in orbit for long periods and then to pounce upon and destroy enemy radar systems when they began emitting.

aircraft, so every Jester airman in the room was an ace.

Johnson and Elton led the scoreboard with seven kills, and Pat Harris and Mike Gurth were second with six kills. In just two days, all had become battle hardened veterans—steel forged in the fires of war.

And that is the way it is in war, Johnson reflected—you measure up instantly when challenged to perform, or you are gone, maybe transferred out of the combat zone, more likely taken out forever by an enemy fighter pilot. This is why training for war is so important.

"After two days and nights of fighting," Falatchik began, "we now have good information on where their emitters are." He confidently displayed information, nomenclature and locations of SAM and antiaircraft sites. Three sites, Johnson noted, guarded Peenemunde, spread to cover the entire complex. Falatchik also indicated the tanker rendezvous point. It was in a relatively safe area west of Koblenz. He also gave them the IFF squawk code for that part of the mission. They would fly the low level portion of the mission with the IFF in Standby. When he had finished, Colonel Johnson gave a general operations briefing. Take-off time was set for 0445. Johnson and Elton went into a flight planning room to work up the details for their flight, and the other three crews went to a different room to plan and coordinate their operations.

"We'll need more fuel than we've been carrying," Johnson said. "We'll have to add at least one centerline tank."

"Roger," said Elton. "Let's do some tight figuring." They drew their course line, angling northeast across East Germany, at one point passing within 30 miles of Berlin. There, embattled American, French and British forces were holding out in the enclave, completely surrounded by Soviet forces.

After the refueling, they planned an almost straight line course past Paderborn, northwest of Kassel, to a point on the West German Air Defense Identification Zone opposite Wolfsburg on the border. Then they would turn straight east, skirting Wolfsburg, crossing the border and heading for a point on the Weser-Elbe Canal. There they would angle northeast again, fly to the Elbe River itself, and follow its course due north for a short time. From there, they would follow a zigzag route across the now flattening terrain, approaching Peenemunde from a point directly south of the test base.

In hopes of concealing their real target until the last possible moment, they would then feint towards a highly restricted area in which it was rumored the Soviets carried out nerve gas experiments. But just short of the restricted area, they would break hard right and attack the giant aircraft at Peenemunde. The distance was, indeed, 430 miles.

185

"Do we have enough JP-4 for this mission? On the deck?" Elton asked. Together, they worked out the figures. "Let's see. We have conformal tanks, a centerline 610-gallon tank, two Mavericks for killing the Myira and four Sidewinders to knock out air defenders." They figured drag indexes for their external stores and consulted the flight planning charts. "We'll make it, but it will be tight," Johnson concluded. "We could carry two wing tanks instead of the centerline, but we'd just have to punch them off if we got into a hassle, so let's go with what we've got."

After more detailed flight planning, Elton transferred the information into the Data Transfer Module. They were finished. At 0230, they met with the other Jesters for the final briefing. Pat Harris showed Johnson the pattern of Tacit Rainbows his three aircraft would establish. Nine of the little cruise-type missiles would be concentrated over the last portion of the route, three in the vicinity of each of the sites defending Peenemunde.

At Peenemunde, the Soviet An-225 crew had been up since 0200, readying the monster six-engined plane for its first operational flight in the combat zone. "Comrades, we are about to undertake the most important mission of this war," said Colonel Ivan Ulevich, the mission commander. "We take off at dawn. When we have blasted the NATO forces with our microwave energy transmitter, we will have neutralized all enemy air support and all radio communications. Without direction and the ability to coordinate operations, they will be defeated by the forces of the Motherland." His voice echoed through the huge hangar in which the Myira was parked as technicians performed final tweaking of the electronics.

"How much longer before we are able to move

out of this hangar?" he asked the technicians, looking back toward the open hangar door. The cold, damp Baltic air wafted through, chilling everyone around the huge Myira. He did not feel comfortable with this vital warfighting system confined to a hangar.

"About two hours, comrade, I think," one of the scientists replied. "But isn't the aircraft safer here, in the hangar, in the event of attack?"

"Not really," Colonel Ulevich replied. "If we were on the ramp, with the crew strapped in, we could start engines and be off the ground in less than five minutes. In this position, we must be pushed backwards out of the hangar. Then we have to start engines and taxi across the ramp, down the taxiway and onto the runway for takeoff. That takes more time. Speed up this technical work so we can get out of here!"

"We will do our best," the technician replied.

Back at Bitburg, the Jesters suited up and boarded the bread truck. They were driven to their aircraft, dispersed but parked as a flight on the ramp. Tom walked over to Harris' Strike Eagle. Like the other supporting Jester aircraft, it was not fitted with a belly tank because it was flying a shorter mission than the one Johnson and Elton were flying to Peenemunde.

The AGM-136s, three to a station, were on launchers on the two wing stations, 2 and 8, and another launcher under the Strike Eagle's belly, behind the LANTIRN pods. Each missile's wing had been rotated 90 degrees and stowed snugly under the missile so it was aligned longitudinally with the missile's fuselage. When launched, the wing would rotate and snap into normal position to provide the lift the missile needed for flight. Electrical power and attack information were being fed to each missile's "brain," its on-board computer, by an umbilical cord from ground support equipment. The operation was completed quickly. Johnson nodded approvingly.

He returned to his own bird and strapped in. There was little time to wait or rest. Time to go. The whole flight started engines at the pre-briefed time and taxied out. This time, Pat Harris and Mike Gurth were in the first aircraft. Two more followed, and Tom and Dick brought up the rear. The Jesters made single ship take-offs at 10-second intervals. Johnson and Elton watched each Jester bird ahead of them take position on the runway, run up engines, release brakes and disappear into the gloom. They followed suit and were soon airborne.

As soon as their own aircraft broke ground, Tom retracted the landing gear and flaps and rolled into a climbing right turn. The Strike Eagle punched into the low overcast. At that speed, they quickly popped out on top at 10,000 feet. A full moon shone down through a clear sky, sketching the F-15E's shadow on the flat cloud bank below. Stars gleamed like small beacons

Peenemunde area as seen on the aerial charts at 1:250,000 scale. Note the absence of towns and villages nearby.

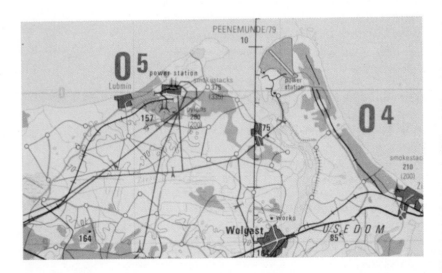

in the night. What a great night for flying. The scene was beautiful and, like any aircraft on a night flight, the Strike Eagle seemed to purr along. The air was soft as velvet. The war seemed far away, but Johnson and Elton could feel its reality, just below the overcast to the east. Elton began searching on radar for their tanker. It was supposed to be north of their position at 20,000 feet.

Johnson had set up the IFF before take-off. Now he checked the settings, on the panel to the left and behind the throttle quadrant. They would be interrogating the tanker using Mode 4, the crypto selective identification feature mode. Elton soon picked out a target that was where the tanker should be. "Got a bogey," he said. He moved the acquisition symbols over the blip on the display and depressed the acquisition button to designate. "That's him, at 11 o'clock, slightly high, 20 miles." He put the radar back in search mode.

Johnson thumbed the AAI interrogate button on the inboard throttle. Both airmen watched the radar display. A circle appeared, superimposed on the target. "Bingo," Johnson said. "That's a high confidence crypto reply." He knew the tanker was interrogating the Strike Eagle's IFF and getting the same results. He reduced the airspeed to 300 knots for the rendezvous. There would be no radio chatter. The pilots in both aircraft, as prebriefed, now placed their IFF systems in Standby.

Johnson held his course straight north. The tanker continued south, its track offset to the west of Johnson's. Silently, Tom and Dick watched as the tanker's symbol moved from 11 o'clock to 10 o'clock. When the two aircraft were 12 miles apart, with the tanker 30 degrees off the Strike Eagle's nose, the tanker pilot began his turn for the rendezvous.

189

KC-10 Extender aircraft exploited the basic DC-10 airframe and engine combination, turning it into a first-class combination aerial tanker and cargo lifter. KC-10 can refuel aircraft of all NATO nations.

"The start of a perfect joinup," commented Tom. When the tanker had completed 90 degrees of turn, they could see it, now between 10 and 11 o'clock, slightly above their altitude, dimly illuminated by the moonlight. It was a big McDonnell Douglas KC-10, equipped to refuel three receivers at a time, one from drogues at each wingtip and one from the boom just under the tail. Tonight, the lone Strike Eagle would refuel from the tail boom.

Both aircraft were flying with all external lights off. Elton placed the radar in Standby. Johnson reached forward, just in front and to the left of the throttle quadrant, and moved the inflight refueling slipway door switch to "open." A "ready" light illuminated on the canopy bow next to the "shoot" light. At the leading edge of the left wing root, just outboard of the engine, the small door covering the refueling receptacle silently slid open. A small light gleamed inside the opening, a beacon for the refueling boom operator in the tanker. They could not see him yet, but would in just a few seconds.

Silently, they watched the distance between the two aircraft diminish as the tanker's turn carried it to their twelve o'clock position. The tanker pilot rolled out wings level exactly in front of the Strike Eagle, which Tom had flown to a position 50 feet beneath and just behind the tanker's tail. The delicate refueling operation was about to begin.

"Right on the mark," said Tom. He could see two rows of lights on the KC-10's belly. One row signalled him to move forward or backward, the other to climb or descend. They would keep him within the refueling envelope—the maneuver limits—of the boom. Until the Strike Eagle was hooked up, the lights were operated manually by the boom operator. Tom could see him, illuminated by the lights of his instrument panel, behind his little window in the belly of the tanker. As soon as they made contact—when the boom operator had inserted the probe into the Strike Eagle's receptacle— the lights would begin to signal automatically, actuated by the position of the boom. Tom took great pride, like most fighter pilots, in keeping the green light illuminated in both rows by holding position exactly.

He advanced the throttles slightly and smoothly moved upward and then forward. Delicately, he reduced power slightly to stabilize his position a few feet behind and below the boom. He stayed slightly offset to the right of the tanker's centerline to put his refueling receptacle exactly in line with the boom. The boom operator, actuating the "wings" near the lower end of the boom, flew it slowly down towards the Strike Eagle, at the same time extending the refueling probe. Tom maintained position by reference to the KC-10, not the boom, but he watched the probe with his peripheral vision. The boom's left wingtip seemed to loom over the canopy bow. Smoothly,

191

slowly, the probe extended and entered the refueling receptacle. There was a slight "clunk" sound and the refueling ready light went out. Both green lights on the tanker's belly blinked on. The Strike Eagle was right in the groove.

Tom, intently watching the KC-10, flicked a glance at the fuel gauges. Fuel levels were coming up as the JP-4 surged from tanker to fighter.

Slowly, the tanker rolled into a 20 degree left bank. Tom flew perfect formation and rolled left a split second later, letting the Strike Eagle slide slightly right to stay in the same plane with the tanker's boom, which now extended at 20 degrees right of vertical. After 180 degrees of turn, the tanker rolled out, and so did Tom. They sailed serenely through the sky, jet fuel singing through the connection.

When the tanks were full, the probe disconnected automatically in a small white puff of fuel vapor. Tom glanced upward at the silent shadow of the boomer behind the window in the KC-10's refueling compartment and mouthed a silent "Thanks." He knew the boomer couldn't see his lips behind the mask, but the man popped him a salute and a thumbs up. Then he lowered the nose and banked toward the east, at the same time closing the refueling door. "Nice job," commented Elton.

They descended through the overcast, entered the clear air below, and dropped down to the deck. They had selected a cruise speed of 450 knots, and Johnson held it exactly. For the first part of the trip, in West Germany, he entrusted the bird to the automatic terrain following system, saving his energy and concentration power for the hard part, manual terrain following under fire in East Germany.

By the time Jester One-One reached the turning point to enter East Germany, Pat Harris had

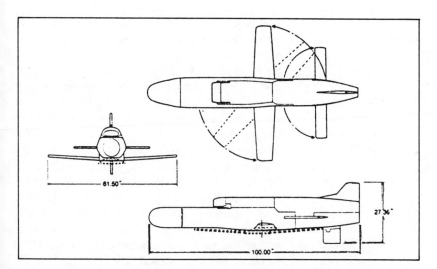

already penetrated deep into enemy airspace on the deck, and was zooming to start deploying his Tacit Rainbow missiles. The other two Jester aircraft had already released their weapons.

When Harris' finger actuated the pickle button, the first missile was ejected from its mount on the Strike Eagle. The missile's "brain," a small computer, had been active since engine startup at Bitburg. Using information fed to it electronically before leaving the ramp, it kept track of its present position and the relative bearing to its loiter point. As soon as it was launched, the computer sent signals to the wing actuator, which swivelled the wing into place in less than a second. In the launch sequence, other flying and control surfaces deployed. Inside the craft, the miniature Williams WR 36-1 turbofan engine started and automatically revved up to full thrust.

Orienting itself by reference to the earth's magnetic field, doppler return and other inputs, the little unmanned aircraft—a flying "smart bomb" that weighed in at 500 pounds, including warhead—banked precisely to its ingress heading

Tacit Rainbow AGM-136 aircraft can be carried by all USAF and USN/USMC fighter and attack aircraft. After launch, it loiters until it finds and homes on enemy radars.

193

and flew, swiftly and whisper-quiet, to its loiter point. There it entered a slow orbit, turning in a silent circle. Its sensors were attuned for the first Soviet radar emission from below. On the ground and in the air, in the blackness, Soviet air defense crews manned their scopes and displays, but none detected the Tacit Rainbows launched by the Jesters.

"Here we go," Johnson said. Turning into enemy territory west of Wolfsburg, Johnson and Elton headed east, flying along one of the old Berlin air approach corridors used during the Cold War. Their sound in the black night immediately attracted antiaircraft fire. But as usual, it was late and off the mark. Frantic sector controllers, staring at blank scopes, ordered defensive fire. Occasionally, bursts fired blind would detonate near the Strike Eagle's flight path, but not close enough to inflict damage. They skirted Wolfsburg to the south and flew east to a point on the Weser-Elbe Canal, where they turned northeast.

"We've got SAM sites in search mode," Elton said, watching the symbology on the TEWS display, "but none of them can paint us for a lockon." They pressed on, Tom banking left and right to avoid "hot spots" he could see through the HUD. They saw wildly firing tracers and AAA bursts behind them.

"We've got an active site at three o'clock," Elton called. At that point, the first Tacit Rainbow performed its mission perfectly. Looking right, the airmen saw a blinding flash as the tungsten fragments of the Tacit Rainbow's exploding warhead knifed into the SAM site with a roar. Dick's TEWS display went blank.

"That's one we won't have to worry about," Johnson commented. Back at the site, surviving crewmen, bewildered, rushed out of their control modules to see what had happened to their antenna and nearby vehicles and installations. There had been no indications on their displays, no sound, no warning. "Do we have a saboteur?" one asked.

The Jester airmen flew on, very low and unseen in the night, to a point south of the town of Stendal and dropped over the west bank of the Elbe, turning sharp left to follow its course north. The river in this area was flanked by levees. Johnson stayed close to the river surface, eyes in the HUD, often climbing slightly to avoid river craft equipped with blackout lights that were cautiously plying the important waterway.

Antiaircraft emplacements on the levees tried snapshots at the sound of the Strike Eagle as it rocketed along. But they were always late, and several equipped with radar were wiped out by Tacit Rainbows.

"So far," Johnson said, "we haven't had to expend any chaff or activate the jamming equipment."

"As far as radar is concerned," Elton said, "we're practically invisible!"

At the point where the Elbe's course angled sharply to the northwest, Johnson broke right and headed northeast, crossing the autobahn from Berlin to Hamburg at a point between two highway fighter strips, Wittstock and Netzeband. Each strip launched a dozen MiG-29s, but the Strike Eagle's radar signature was hidden from their radar displays by the ground clutter.

Also launched that night was Colonel Gorshkov in his MiG-25. He was still smarting from having been shot down twice in two nights. He was more obsessed than ever with killing a Strike Eagle.

Looking to the right, Johnson and Elton could now see the flicker of gunfire on the horizon. Flashes of artillery and bomb bursts from the pitched battle for Berlin simulated the Aurora

Borealis and forecast the daylight soon to come. Elton's TEWS display now showed antiaircraft and SAM activity in all quadrants. Some emissions were silenced abruptly as the AGM-136s, dropping from the skies like thunderbolts, performed their mission. Their F-15E pressed onward, the wash from its low-level flight riffling the river waters.

The Strike Eagle now flashed over the next checkpoint, the middle of a large lake-filled area south of the small city of Neustrelitz. Johnson now rolled right and pointed the nose straight east once again. "It's time to arm 'em up," he said. Elton read off the arming checklist as he scrolled it down one of his displays. Johnson repeated each step, actuating switches as he did so. All armament checked out.

They now angled northeast, to the city of Pasewalk. They were now near the border between East Germany and Poland, and Johnson rolled left to angle across a railroad and highway that paralleled the Baltic coast. The terrain was flat and marshy below them and there were ZSU-23 tracers and heavier 57mm antiaircraft bursts

196

Weapons technicians installing Tacit Rainbow on a Navy A-6E illustrate missile's size.

punctuated their flight path. Johnson used the HUD to avoid sites he could see. Two SAM sites tried to lock on. The first one was taken out by a Tacit Rainbow. The second launched a SAM, but Elton released a packet of chaff to confuse it. Before another SAM could be launched, the site was taken out by another AGM-136. Elton and Johnson thanked their robotic buddies.

They now flashed over the western extreme of the large body of water southeast of Peenemunde known as the Oderhaff, and a smaller one called the Peenestrom. An antiaircraft projectile burst right over the cockpit, causing both men to duck. There was a crackling sound of rushing air as a fragment of twisted steel pierced the clear plastic canopy over Elton's head. Now Johnson banked hard left, making his feint towards the Restricted Area. He shoved the throttles to full military power and pulled up to 500 feet.

In the big hangar at Peenemunde, Colonel Ulevich heard the staccato firing of the ZSU-23s, the heavier crump of 57mm antiaircraft shells detonating, and the unfamiliar, heavier roar of the AGM-136s impacting into their targets. His instincts told him he was about to be taken under air attack. His senses confirmed the thought. He reacted immediately. "Into the Myira! Start engines! Push us out onto the ramp!" he ordered.

He ran up the narrow stairs to the flight deck. In the dim light, he saw the flight engineer, seated at the massive flight engineer's panel running along the right side of the cockpit behind the pilots, was already responding to the pilot's orders. "Starting Number Four." He watched his CRT and instruments for the right inboard engine as it began to rotate and the RPM, temperature and pressure indicators began to come up.

"Hurry! Hurry! Hurry!" shouted Colonel Ulevich.

Aboard the streaking F-15E, Elton switched the

radar out of Standby. The APG-70's antenna made three sweeps before he put the set into Freeze mode. Rapidly but carefully, he scrutinized the radar picture. At this close range it was as good as a black and white photograph. He saw the long runway, running northwest-southeast. Several large hangars and a power plant sat on the south side of the base. There was another power plant, a bigger one, directly east of the base, across the body of water that separated Peenemunde from the mainland.

Peenemunde was now at their three o'clock position. The air under the perennial overcast was clear. Although the base was blacked out, both airmen could see the smokestacks of the power stations jutting into the air, and the blinking of ship navigation buoys offshore in the Baltic.

"Now!" Johnson called, and racked the bird into a vertical right bank, rolling back level when the nose pointed directly at the target.

"Can you identify the Myira?" Johnson asked.

Elton was still studying the radar picture. "I don't see it. Could it be in one of the hangars?"

"I don't think so. Too damn big." Johnson paused. The target area was now fifteen seconds away. The Mavericks were armed. "We'll fly right over the hangar area and I'll look for it with the LANTIRN."

"What about terminal defenses?" Elton reminded him.

"We didn't come all this way just to blow up a couple of buildings. We're going to get that big sonofabitch!"

In the Myira, startup continued. "Starting Number three," the flight engineer intoned. With two engines started, Ulevich gave orders to the tug starting to push the huge aircraft backward. "Speed up, faster," he bellowed.

Now the Strike Eagle roared over the field

boundary at 500 knots, 100 feet off the deck.
Johnson stared through the HUD, which showed
him the ramp and hangars, bright as day. He
ignored the tracers flashing over the cockpit and
sat snug in his seat as the bird bounced from
the concussion of near AAA misses. The gunners
were coming so close that both airmen could
hear the PUM! PUM! PUM! of projectiles exploding
around them. A pall of smoke began to settle
over the airdrome as flak filled the sky.

As always, Elton had the HUD picture on one
of his displays. He studied it intently. Then he
saw it—the tail of the huge bird was sticking
out of one of the hangars! The Myira's rudder
had been just too tall to get into the hangar while
work was being done inside. The huge 101-foot
tailplanes and 59-foot high rudder gave it away.

199

"There it is! The big hangar on the left!" he
called out.

"Rog—I see it!" Johnson said. He put the bird
in a hard, 9.0-G left turn, grunting loudly to help
his body fight the G forces. They flashed out
over the Baltic, wings vertical, and Tom brought
the nose around for the kill. Now tracers converged
toward them. They seemed to flash like big,
lethal, lazy arrows aimed toward the windscreen.
He ignored them as they zipped by, over and
under the Strike Eagle. Mavericks One and Two
were selected and ready. He flew the aircraft to
superimpose the aircraft velocity vector over the
aiming point. He designated the target for the
missiles as it came into their field of view.

Colonel Ulevich felt the Myira start to move
backward onto the ramp. Only a few more
seconds, and he could disconnect the tug and
taxi under the power of his six Lotarev D-18
turbo fan engines.

"Look!" Johnson said, as more of the enormous
Myira's long fuselage emerged, backlit by the

lights inside the hangar. "They're trying to back that thing out of the hangar!"

The range caret followed its track down the side of the HUD display. It was halfway between max and min range. The Shoot cues began to flash on the display and in the top of the canopy bow. Firmly, Johnson thumbed the button on the stick. Twice.

Both missiles leaped off their launchers a second apart in a flash of fire, and sped unerringly to their target. Johnson turned 30 degrees off the attack heading to start the escape maneuver. Both men twisted their heads around to watch the results. The first missile punched through the thin fuselage skin ahead of the Ruslan's tail. Its warhead detonated inside the microwave energy transmission compartment, slashing and blasting the equipment to ribbons of junk. Bodies of technicians and scientists were blown through the forward compartment bulkhead.

The second Maverick blasted into the Myira farther forward, near the wing root, shattering one of the main spars. The huge wing flopped down and the tip scraped the concrete ramp. The gargantuan aircraft stopped moving. Fragments of the warhead penetrated the fuel tanks and the flight deck.

There was a momentary delay, and then huge explosions erupted. Colonel Ulevich took fragments through the heart and head, and the men of his flight crew leaped to escape the flames. Fire shot up through the roof of the building. Orange and red flames leaped up, and black smoke boiled up in a column that quickly reached to the overcast. Other explosions followed. The bottom of the overcast glowed red, reflecting the inferno below.

The tail of the Myira slowly sagged earthward as the gargantuan aircraft and its equipment were twisted and melted by the heat. Support equipment inside the hangar burned fiercely as the Soviet firefighting crews began to move from their station across the ramp. The Soviet microwave energy threat was destroyed.

"We got it!" Johnson exclaimed. "Now, let's get the hell out of here!" Descending back to the deck, Tom pointed the nose west southwest, in the direction of the West German border. He retarded the throttles to hold 350 knots, an airspeed that economized fuel. Pursued by unseeing air defenders, including the frustrated Colonel Gorshkov, the Strike Eagle flew across the border at Lubeck and landed at a German field near Hamburg. German ground crewmen, trained to service aircraft of all NATO nations, quickly refueled the Strike Eagle. After checking the superficial battle damage, Johnson and Elton decided to fly home. They returned to Bitburg before dawn. The other three Jesters had returned safely.

Confrontation

Strike Eagles vs. Foxbats at 25,000 feet

As usual, Colonel Crawford and Sergeant Collins were waiting when they taxied down the ramp and rolled to a stop in their parking spot at Bitburg. Crawford was smiling, elated they had once again accomplished their mission. Jennifer Collins placed the chocks in front of the main gear, then scanned the aircraft for damage. She was happy but inquisitive as Tom backed down the ladder.

"Get any more MiGs, Colonel?" she asked.

"Not this time, Jennifer," Tom replied, taking the maintenance book from her and completing the blocks for this mission.

Jennifer tried to hide her disappointment that they had not gotten some more Soviet kills, more stars to paint on her aircraft.

"Nobody's perfect," Tom told her. "Maybe next time we'll be luckier." She nodded, then mounted the ladder to the front cockpit, to begin the task of preparing the plane for its next mission.

The two airmen were bone tired. As Crawford drove them toward Operations, he briefed them on the current war situation. "We think the tide is turning. Their ground attack has stalled. We have racked up a six to one kill ratio in the air. Back in the Pentagon, they are generating a slew of messages to the CINCs, urging a heavy push everywhere today. SACEUR doesn't need all that help from the people in the NMCC at the Pentagon. He's getting the support he needs from the NATO council."

Tom chuckled. "They must be having a ball in the NMCC; an actual war to monitor."

Crawford replied, "Yeah, that's true. You and I both did time in the Puzzle Palace. But SACEUR is calling the shots over here. He wants an all-out combined attack to start pushing them back. We're putting up a maximum effort this afternoon and you're part of the package."

Both airmen sat up straight, their fatigue now forgotten.

"We're going to fight in the daytime?" Elton asked. "Isn't that against union rules?"

Crawford smiled at the insider joke. "You Jesters do your best work at night, I know. But now you're going to do some day fighter work. SACEUR says we must establish air supremacy today so the ground pounders can do their job right. So we're putting up everything that has an air-to-air capability, including F-15Es. I want you to get some sleep. You will be joining your flight for the briefing at 1100."

They walked out of the command post, hit the field cafeteria and wolfed down breakfast. They headed for the BOQ. Two hours of sleep would restore the edge they needed.

Across the FEBA at Haina, Colonel Gorshkov landed his MiG-25. He was met with the news that a large NATO air attack was expected sometime during the day. The expectation was based on Soviet intelligence reports of an early morning standdown at NATO air bases. Frenzied ground

203

Key rooms at the National Military Command Center (NMCC) in the Pentagon. Nerve center for worldwide US military operations, it is seldom as empty and unpopulated as in these photos. Secretary of Defense is briefed in room in photo above; operations staffs work in room shown at right above.

activity was reported at all the Allied air bases. He briefed the survivors of his wing.

"Comrades, we must be ready to repel this attack and enable our ground and air forces to keep pressure on the enemy. We have lost many fighters and will lose more. But we must fight to the death for the Motherland. We must be prepared to make the supreme sacrifice, using our aircraft as weapons if we have to."

Gorshkov harked back to his youth, when he had first started military flying. As part of his training, he had learned of the Soviet propensity to ram other aircraft in combat. The taran, it was called, and it had worked many times on the German-Russian front. "Yes, comrades, we must

even be prepared to execute the taran, as our predecessors have done. You have been taught about Senior Lieutenant I.M. Polyakov. He became a gold star Hero of the Soviet Union in the Great Patriotic War. Like Polyakov, we must all be prepared to take extreme measures in defense of the Motherland."

He knew, and so did they, that Polyakov got the Hero medal posthumously. He pretended to ignore a few snickers which came from some of the younger pilots who had racked up kills during the last three days. They all knew he had flown twice and been shot down twice. Most of them thought he was too old for fighters and should have retired years ago. But he did not think he was too old, and was determined to prove his supremacy once again in battle. No matter what it took. After his briefing, all the Soviet pilots retired for a few hours sleep.

At Bitburg, all aircrews were in their places in the briefing room early and the briefers started at 1100 sharp. In East Germany, Soviet pilots were getting their briefings, too.

"You'll take off in flights of four, climb to altitude fast and head for East Germany," Colonel Crawford said. It was expected, he went on, that scores of aircraft would be pitted against each other in the battle for air superiority. Other briefers followed assigning tracks and airspace by flight. The Jesters drew an area right over Fulda.

Johnson briefed his flight thoroughly and led them into Personal Equipment, where they donned flight gear. They headed out to the Strike Eagles, again dispersed but parked together on the wet ramp as a flight. Armament for the air-to-air mission was a mixture of ordnance for aerial combat: four Sidewinder heatseekers and four AMRAAM radar guided missiles, and 500 rounds

At Bitburg Air Base, an F-15 taxis for takeoff in a prewar photo. Once the war began, the taxiway was often used as a tactical airstrip while the main runway, 06-24, was repaired after being cratered by attacks by Su-24 and Su-25 aircraft.

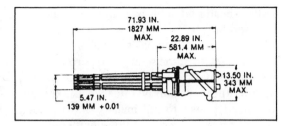

20mm Vulcan gun nestles in F-15's right wing root. Its six rotating barrels spew high velocity projectiles at extraordinary rate of 6,000 rounds per minute.

of high explosive incendiary ammunition for the M61A1 Vulcan gun.

As the second hand passed through the 12 o'clock position on his G.I. watch, Johnson extended his hand above his head and made a circular motion with his index finger. The jet starters on all four Jester birds moaned to life. When all cockpit and seat safety pins had been removed and crew chiefs had pulled the chocks, they taxied out, passed through the arming and quick check areas and took the runway. Johnson taxied into the number one position a few hundred feet down the runway, left of the centerline. Number two, Sandy Scott, took his left wing, in a staggered position on the left hand side of the runway. Pat Harris, Number three and alternate lead, lined up on Tom's right wing, just to the right of the centerline, and number four lined up on Pat's right wing. It was good to be flying together.

Tom firmly depressed the rudder pedals to hold the brakes and gave the engine runup signal, twirling his index finger. Everybody advanced his throttles to 80 percent and checked instrument readings. Each man looked over the aircraft next to him to be sure flaps were set correctly and there were no leaks or loose panels. Tom looked at his wingman, who nodded his head almost imperceptibly to indicate he was ready to roll. Tom looked right and got two more head nods. He then looked straight down the runway, gave a sharp head nod of his own and simultaneously released brakes.

Tom advanced the throttles to full military power and then retarded the setting two percent to give his wingman some room for power adjustments. Simultaneously, Sandy released brakes and advanced power to full military. As one, both aircraft started to move. With only the air-to-air missiles on board, the lightly loaded Strike Eagles lunged down the runway and almost leaped off the ground. Sandy held his position by making slight power adjustments. When he saw Tom's nosewheel strut starting to extend, he pulled back on the stick and started his own nose up. As the two aircraft came off the ground together, Sandy immediately reached for the gear handle. His wheels retracted at the same time as Tom's, followed immediately by the flaps coming up.

Pat, in the Number three position, waited ten seconds and, with a nod, started his own two-ship element rolling down the runway. Their takeoff was a carbon copy of the first.

Tom held the runway heading for twenty seconds and started a 30-degree banked right turn. He retarded the throttles to hold 300 knots for the joinup. Sandy now moved with Tom, but stacked down because he was on the inside of the turn. As soon as Pat was a safe distance above the ground, he also rolled into a right turn with a slightly steeper angle of bank than Tom's. He also held 300 knots in the turn, but actually was gaining on Tom by flying a shorter distance in the tighter turn. When he had reached a point along an imaginary line from Tom's aircraft through his close formation position, Sandy stopped his overtake and began to shallow his bank to move up the imaginary line towards Tom. As the four aircraft reached 180 degrees of turn, Pat and his wingmen had reached a perfect close formation

position. Johnson, with the flight members following, rolled out wings level and entered the bottom of the everpresent overcast. When every plane was in position, Tom pointed to his helmet and held up four fingers. All four aircrews switched to Channel Four, the AWACS frequency.

Brains of the F-15: a trained fighter pilot with wingman nearby in loose formation, heading for the attack.

"Jester Flight, Check."

"Toop."

"Three."

"Four."

Tom kept his flight in close formation until they popped out on top of the overcast, and then moved his rudder pedals back and forth to fishtail his aircraft. This was the signal to go to the Jesters' attack formation. Immediately, the other three aircraft banked slightly away from Tom and moved quickly and smoothly into positions that were almost abreast of Tom, with about 2,000 feet between aircraft. They were now climbing through 25,000 feet.

"Sentinel, Jester One-One with four," Johnson radioed.

"Jester One-One, Sentinel. Turn to 070. Your

F-15C of Bitburg wing, armed for air to air combat. When developed, the F-15 was to be an air superiority fighter, with "not a pound for air to ground" attack roles. F-15E Strike Eagle changed that, making the aircraft a true multirole fighter.

targets 12 o'clock, 60 miles, Flight Level 260."

"I've got six bogeys, 12 o'clock, 55 miles," Elton said on intercom.

"Rog, I see 'em," Johnson replied. "Sentinel, Jester One-One has radar contact. Jesters, Arm 'em up." He selected air-to-air on the Master Mode switch beneath the HUD, called up his missile displays, actuated the Master Arm switch and made sure the thumb switch on the inboard side of the right throttle was in the forward, or MRM position, to be ready to fire his AMRAAMs.

Battles between flights of four and six aircraft per side were shaping up all along the FEBA. The distance between flights rapidly diminished as adversaries approached each other at closing

211

speeds of more than 1,200 knots.

The six Soviet fighters approaching the Jester flight were MiG-25 Foxbats, led by Colonel Gorshkov.

He picked up the Jesters on his radar just after his flight had been designated a target for the Jesters. Now, he would have a chance to realize his ambition to shoot down an American fighter, preferably an F-15E. The adrenalin coursed through his body as he checked his four Aphid heatseeker missiles. They would be ready and so would he.

The Jesters had an immediate advantage over Gorshkov. He and his flight carried only heat-seekers, while the Jesters carried both radar-guided and heatseeker missiles. Their AMRAAMs were deadly in a head-on attack while Gorshkov's AA-11 Archers were less effective head-on. Also, the AMRAAM had a longer range. Each Jester picked out the Soviet fighter opposite him on the scope and prepared to attack.

They rushed toward each other. At 10 miles, with the display showing he was in range, Tom launched his first AMRAAM. It flew off the rail and sped towards Gorshkov's wingman. He broke hard right, forcing the aircraft on his right to break also. Tom's AMRAAM flew true and blew the wing off the MiG-25. Now the 10 aircraft merged into a swirling mass. Everyone turned hard to stay with a target. "Jester Lead, break right!" Sandy called. "MiG at your five o'clock!" Tom racked his bird into a 9.0-G turn. The MiG tried to turn with him and was sucked right in front of Sandy, who launched a Sidewinder up his tailpipe. The aircraft exploded and the pilot ejected.

Gorshkov came around in a hard left turn and almost collided with Tom head on. The two aircraft flashed past each other, missing by ten feet. Gorshkov headed after Sandy. He launched one of his missiles, which did not track its target. Frustrated, he launched a second one out of range. It fizzled and dropped. At that point, he drifted in front of Pat Harris, who was pursuing another MiG. The range was only 1,500 feet, so Pat thumbed the weapons select switch from "MRM" to "Gun," and saw the Air-to-Air gun attack symbology appear on the HUD. He superimposed the aiming pipper on Gorshkov's MiG-25 and depressed the trigger on the stick. The Gatling gun in the right wing root belched out a solid stream of steel. The rounds blasted into the target and chewed off Gorshkov's wingtip. He broke hard left to get out of the line of fire. Pat started left, then heeded a "Break right" command from

Tom, so that engagement was broken off. Two more MiGs, meanwhile, were plunging earthward trailing smoke and fire.

Everyone was "hooking" now, turning hard into the fight, creating the proverbial "furball" that supposedly has been obsolete since World War Two, but that has developed in every major air engagement since. Johnson blasted straight through the developing furball and hooked hard back in. Elton grunted loudly against the Gs and called "MiG at three o'clock!" Instinctively, Tom broke hard toward the MiG, which had bored in close. It was Gorshkov, who unleashed his third missile. But he was too close and the missile did not have time to arm before it passed close over Tom's cockpit and disappeared without detonating. Gorshkov was cursing his luck again. As the two aircraft passed each other, Gorshkov caught sight of the harlequin mask on the side of Tom's aircraft. A Jester aircraft again! He would get this bastard at all costs!

Gorshkov kept sight of Tom's aircraft as Tom pursued one of the remaining MiGs. Tom

213

First production F-15E, loaded with air-to-air missiles.

When it's time to eject, this is the sequence of events. Thanks to ejection seats, aircrew members from both sides of the conflict survived to fly again.

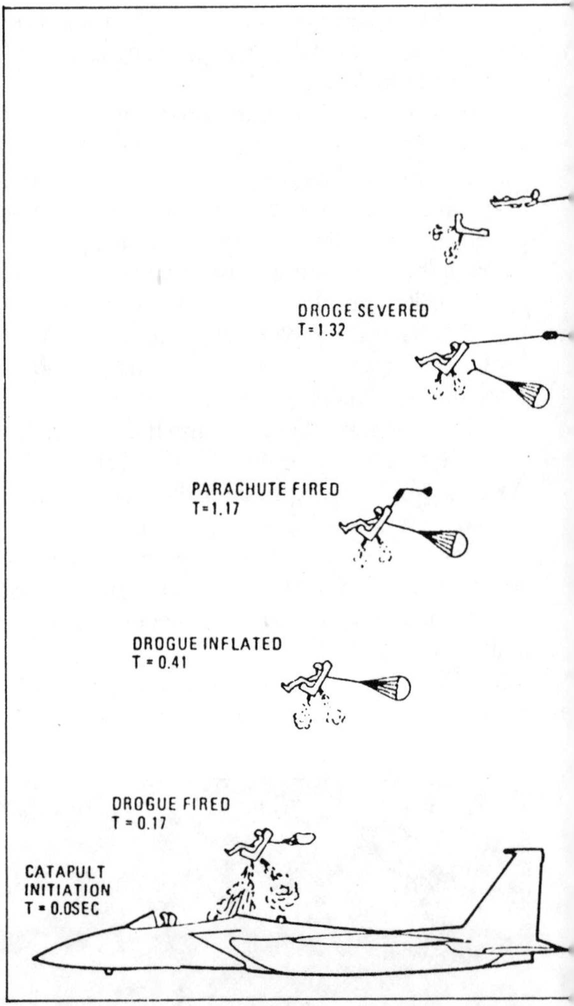

214

DROGE SEVERED
T=1.32

PARACHUTE FIRED
T=1.17

DROGUE INFLATED
T = 0.41

DROGUE FIRED
T = 0.17

CATAPULT
INITIATION
T = 0.0SEC

maneuvered into the MiG's rear quarter, thumbed the weapon select switch to the center "SRM" position and pressed the nose gear steering button on the stick to uncage the seeker head of the Sidewinder. He heard the tone in his headset and depressed the pickle button on the stick. The Sidewinder whooshed away, locked onto

FULL INFLATION
T = 2.90

the MiG.

Gorshkov was now in range. Now or never. He fired his last heatseeker. It did not guide precisely to its target but detonated at the edge of its lethal envelope. Shrapnel from the AA-11 warhead spattered the Strike Eagle. Several pieces slashed through the side of the rear cockpit. They ricocheted off the top of the instrument panel and were imbedded in Dick Elton's chest. Tom heard the roar of the detonation, felt the concussion, and almost simultaneously heard the sound of ripping metal and then rushing air. There was no sound from Dick Elton.

"Dick! Dick! You okay?" Elton had been knocked unconscious and his head slumped to his chest. In his mirrors Tom could see blood spattered over the inside of the canopy. Tom began a turn toward home. He assumed Dick was alive, but possibly bleeding to death. The nearest base—and a hospital—was Bitburg.

Gorshkov was now in a fury. He'd fired his last shot and the hated Jester aircraft was still flying. But he had vowed to get a Strike Eagle kill.

216

What to do now? In the back of his brain, the thought of ramming asserted itself again. Was this not the time to try it? He had never heard of the taran being executed in a jet aircraft, but he had no weapons left. He had a choice of leaving the fray without a kill, or of using his aircraft as a weapon. It would be worth it, he decided, especially since the aircraft he was after was from the hated Jester squadron.

Johnson was now in a left bank, turning for home. Gorshkov moved his throttles into afterburner range, high above Tom, and moved out ahead and to his right. Then he brought his MiG-25 around in a tight turn, rolled in steeply and started his dive, leveling off to come at Tom from the front quarter.

"Jester One-One! Bogey at one o'clock!" called Sandy. But he was too late. At the last instant, Tom saw the MiG, so close it looked as big as a bomber. Before he could react, Gorshkov's fuselage was ripping into Tom's raised right wing. There was a horrendous crash and the sound of tearing metal. The Strike Eagle yawed sharply to the right as Gorshkov's aircraft ripped away almost the entire right wing. Gorshkov's aircraft began to descend, trailing fire. Tom's wing had gashed the fuel tanks and one of the engines. For the third time, Gorshkov ejected.

When the Strike Eagle yawed right, Johnson instinctively stomped left rudder to bring the nose back. Then he had to use full left stick to keep the aircraft from rolling to the right and apply hard right rudder to keep the nose from turning left. When he had brought the aircraft under control, he looked back at the right wing to assess the damage. His jaw dropped. There was no right wing outboard of the engine nacelle! The jagged edges of the composite layered

Ultimate survivor. This F-15 was rammed by an enemy aircraft and most of its right wing was sheared off. The pilot managed to keep the airplane flying, a tribute to his skill and its design. He brought it home to land and be repaired to fly again.

217

graphite stuck out in the slipstream. There was a loud roaring from the right side of the aircraft and the sound of air rushing through the rear cockpit. Cockpit pressurization was gone, but the triple redundant flight control system seemed to be working perfectly. The aircraft was still flying.

"Dick! Dick! Are you still with me?" A low moan came over the intercom. He was alive! Now Tom lowered the nose and headed for home.

"Sentinel, Jester One-One. I'm RTB. Please inform Eifel control I have serious battle damage and a wounded man on board."

"Roger, Jester One-One."

Tom switched to Bitburg Tower. The tower was calling him. "Jester One-One, what are your intentions?"

"I'm missing almost all of my right wing. I'm going to give this thing a controllability check and try to land it."

"Roger, standing by."

Leveling at 10,000 feet, Tom began to slow the aircraft to determine if he could control it at traffic pattern speeds. After experimenting for several minutes, he called. "Bitburg, this thing is uncontrollable below 275 knots. My backseater is wounded and unconscious. I'm going to bring it in. Clear the runway."

"Jester One-One, did you say TWO seventy-five?"

"Roger. 275."

Colonel Crawford's voice came over the air. "Jester One-One, you don't have much of a chance at 275. Even with arresting gear you'll probably roll that thing up in a ball and kill yourself. Have you considered bailing out?"

"Considered it and rejected it," Tom replied. "I can't leave Dick. I'm going to try an arrested landing on 24."

"Roger," said Crawford. "Give it a try." Tom

knew the odds against him were astronomical. Normal touchdown speed in the F-15E was around 120 knots. He'd be coming in at almost three times that speed. And even if he kept it under control until he was on the ground, he didn't know what would happen then. If he lost it, he and Elton would be dead.

"Dear God," he prayed, "be with me now." Then, for the second time in two days, he told himself, "I've just got to spend more time in church with the family."

Now Tom, still at 10,000 feet, lowered the gear. There was some buffeting, but the aircraft remained controllable. The airspeed was too high to lower the flaps. He descended to traffic pattern altitude and started a long, flat approach. The ground seemed to be rushing by as fast as it did when he was flying at 540 knots at 100 feet.

He lowered the hook for the arresting gear. Carefully, Tom reduced power to lower the airspeed. No good. Below 275 knots, the right wing—or what was left of it—started to drop. The roaring sound was distracting. His throat was dry and he was breathing hard. A cold sweat broke out on his forehead. He thanked God for rudder trim. He could never be able to hold the rudder against the yaw with his leg alone.

The approach lights began to flick by under the nose. He crossed the overrun and then the runway threshold. Almost strangling the stick, he gently flew the aircraft onto the runway. "Don't bounce it," he told himself. "At this speed, a bounce will be fatal." The wheels made contact with an agonizing squeal. He chopped the throttles but did not stopcock them because he needed engine RPM to keep the electrical and hydraulic systems on line.

He felt the tailhook engage the arresting cable and experienced a brief spurt of elation as he was hurled forward in his harness. Then, with a loud clanging sound, the hook tore the arresting gear loose and the deceleration stopped. He careened down the runway at 175 knots. He got on both brakes—hard. The antiskid brakes began cycling, giving the wheels an 80 percent rolling skid, the most effective stopping action.

The fire engines raced down the runway behind him. At full speed, they fell way behind. He watched the markers on the side of the runway flashing by. Six thousand feet to go, 170 knots. Four thousand, 145 knots. Two thousand, 90 knots. Come on, baby, slow down. One thousand, 60 knots. End of runway, 50 knots. Plenty of speed to kill you. Then the aircraft shot across the overrun and halted with the nose gear against the boundary fence.

Wearily, he cut the engines. They wound down. For a short time it was very quiet. Pungent odor of burned rubber was strong. The fire engines and ambulances roared up. They unstrapped Dick Elton and lifted him into an ambulance that roared off, siren screaming, for the hospital.

Colonel Crawford said, "Come on, Tom. I'll drive you over to the hospital." On the way, he told Tom the fighter attack had worked. The back of the Soviet air force was broken for now.

At the hospital, Elton was coming to.

"Can I see him?" Tom asked the doctor, who nodded and stood aside. Tom went into the room.

"Next time," he told Elton, "you better duck."

"Roger that," said Elton. "You, too. I wonder who that guy was and why he tried to ram us."

"Yeah," said Tom. "You'd almost think he was mad at us."

"And he doesn't even know us," responded Elton.

❖

STRIKE EAGLES

Fates of the major characters

Lt. Col. Tom Johnson, commander of the Deadly Jesters, was awarded the Distinguished Flying Cross for his actions in the early days of the conflict. He received a spot promotion to colonel and was reassigned as vice commander, 36th Tactical Fighter Wing, for the campaign into Poland. He became a double ace before being wounded and shot down.

Col. Valerie Gorshkov, flyer and leader in the Aviatsiya PVO, requested and received transfer to lead a MiG-29 air regiment in the next phases of the conflict. He earned the Hero of the Soviet Union medal for his sustained combat leadership.

Lt. Col. Dick Elton was also awarded the Distinguished Flying Cross. After recovery from his wounds, he was reassigned to the Fighter Weapons School at Nellis AFB as chief instructor of air-to-ground tactics.

Col. Van Crawford, commander of the 36th Tactical Fighter Wing, continued leading the wing in air combat for the ensuing campaigns of the conflict in Central Europe. He was shot down and lost over Gdansk after achieving acedom.

Sgt. Jennifer Collins, crew chief. Deployed forward with 461st in the next phase of the conflict. Promoted to Staff Sergeant and line chief for the 461st. Wounded in the Soviet raid on forward operating location at the Poznan/Lawica airfield, she was evacuated to the USAF Hospital at Wiesbaden.

Glossary

Acronyms and Abbreviations

AAA	antiaircraft artillery; flak
AA-11	Archer air to air missile (Soviet)
AA-6	Acrid infrared and radar air to air missile
AA-8	Aphid IR and radar air to air missile
AA-9	Amos radar air to air missile
ADIZ	air defense identification zone
AGM-130	modular precision standoff guided bomb
AGM-136	TACIT RAINBOW unmanned aircraft to kill enemy radar
AHRS	attitude heading reference system
AIM-7	Sparrow radar guided air to air missile
AIM-9	Sidewinder heatseeking air to air missile
ALARS	alternate launch and recovery system with arresting gear; tactical runway
AMRAAM	advanced medium range air to air missile (AIM-120)
An-225	Antonov heavy transport aircraft nicknamed *Myira*

ASE	allowable steering error circle
AWACS	airborne warning and control system in E-3A aircraft
Bogey	enemy aircraft
Bread Wagon	truck that takes aircrews to their aircraft
CINC	commander in chief, as CINCLANT, CINCUSAFE
CINCUSAFE	commander in chief, US Air Forces in Europe
DEFCON	defense readiness condition; alert posture, graded from 5 (peacetime) to 1 (war imminent)
DTM	data transfer module; cartridge with mission data
E and E	escape and evasion
ELINT	electronic intelligence
EUCOM	US European Command; senior US military headquarters
FEBA	forward edge of the battle area
FENCER	Su-24 variable geometry two-seat attack aircraft
FLANKER	Su-27 all-weather fighter
FLIR	forward looking infrared sensor system
FLOT	forward line of troops
FOXBAT	MiG-25 interceptor aircraft
FOXHOUND	MiG-31
FULCRUM	MiG-29 air superiority fighter
HAVE QUICK	UHF antijam radio communication system
HUD	head up display; displays information to pilot at eye level
IAS	indicated airspeed
IFF	identification friend or foe
INS	inertial navigation system; self-contained
IP	initial point; start point for run to the target

JFS	jet fuel starter on F-15 aircraft
JP-4	jet fuel of a certain grade
JTIDS	joint tactical information display system
LANTIRN	low altitude navigation and targeting infrared system for night
Maverick	AGM-65 air to ground missile
MPCD	multipurpose color display
MPD	multipurpose display
MiG	Mikoyan-Gurevich design bureau
MPD	multipurpose display
PRF	pulse repetition frequency (of a radar transmitter)
RWR	radar warning receiver
SACEUR	Supreme Allied Commander, Europe
SAM	surface to air missile
SA-7, etc.	surface to air missile (Soviet)
Su	Sukhoi design bureau
TACAN	UHF air navigation aid; provides bearing and distance data
TAS	true airspeed
TEWS	tactical electronic warning system
TF	terrain following
T/O	takeoff
TSD	tactical situation display on F-15E
TVD	Soviet theater of military operation (*Teatr Voyennykh Deystviy*)
UHF	ultra high frequency radio band, 300-3,000MHz
USAFE	US Air Forces in Europe
VHF	very high frequency band, 30-300 MHz
Wild Weasel	radar suppression aircraft
ZSU-23	Soviet 23mm multibarrel AA gun, radar directed
Zulu	Greenwich mean time

224